WONDERBOY

WONDERBOY

Nicole Burstein

ANDERSEN PRESS • LONDON

First published in 2016 by
Andersen Press Limited
20 Vauxhall Bridge Road
London
SW1V 2SA
www.andersenpress.co.uk

2 4 6 8 10 9 7 5 3 1

British Library Cataloguing in Publication Data available.

ISBN 978 1 78344 446 5

Printed and bound in Great Britain by Clays Limited,
Bungay, Suffolk, NR35 1ED

For my brother James,
always a hero to me.

1

There's no room for superheroes at Gatford House.

In a world with Vigils flying around, you'd think it would be nearly impossible to find yourself in danger. You'd think that everything would be safe and easy, because what would be the point of doing anything bad if you're just going to get caught out by somebody in a cape? I watch the big saves like everybody else, on the news, on YouTube and on the Vigil fansites, and it could be that I've watched too many, because they've left me with the delusion that maybe, perhaps this time, someone will swoop in at the last minute and save me. But of course they don't. Quantum, the leader of the UK team of Vigils, doesn't descend from the sky like a vanquishing angel. Hayley Divine, with her gift for lightning speed, doesn't swoosh around the corner to come to my rescue. Which is why I'm here, cowering behind the school dumpsters, waiting for the boys who are chasing me to pass before I risk shaking up my inhaler.

Godfrey's minions pass by in one rampaging herd, but I wait a beat longer before I dare relax. It feels like there's

1

a boa constrictor wrapped around my chest all the way up to my throat, pulsing and squeezing, but my lungs are going to have to wait another moment, just long enough so that I can be sure the boys have gone, and that I'm safe. My pulse throbs through my fingers and right up into the tips of my ears, but I wait, just a little longer. The holding-on is its own endurance test: how long can I last? How much more can I take? Before finally, excruciatingly, it's like I've been underwater for too long and I absolutely must come up to breathe.

I break the surface and pump the inhaler, gulping the vapour down, and the mind-fog swiftly clears away. I stoop over, my hands on my knees, feeling my strength return, feeling the boa constrictor uncoil and ease off, slithering away with each deep breath I take.

Would you believe that there was a time when I thought that misspelling Hitler as 'Titler' throughout a coursework essay was hilarious? It seems so pathetic now. Godfrey had ordered me to write the history essay for him because he needed a B grade to participate in the rugby match against Queen's, and so far, Godders the Great was only averaging a D. The essay was key to ensuring that Gatford House beat our historic rivals, because without Godders, Gatford was surely doomed. And obviously I had complied. That is my role after all, to always comply with whatever the other kids here want. They don't call me Wilco for nothing.

It was Fat Henry who first came up with the nickname, which is surprising because usually nobody ever listens to Fat Henry. But his dad is in the RAF, and because of that he always comes out with pilot jargon, like he's so cool for knowing that stuff. Apparently 'wilco' is air-force radio shorthand for 'will comply', and after Fat Henry used it to describe me just once, it stuck. The fact that it sounded almost exactly like my last name was just a stupid lucky bonus. Got some homework that needs a spelling and grammar check? Just hand it to Wilco. You can pay with a packet of crisps tomorrow. Need a parent's letter to get you off PE? Wilco will draft it up and forge the signature for the price of letting me push ahead of you in the lunch queue. Want to know what happens in that book you're meant to be reading for English? Wilco will hack the film online and copy it on to a flash drive for the price of...well...not calling me any rude names for a week? In the great food chain of Gatford House, where the sportsy ones are lions and tigers, and the ludicrous rah-rah kids are gazelles, I'm a bug that hides in the grass. But I've sussed out a way to remain uneaten: just do whatever anyone wants. If they ask, you say yes. Always, no exceptions. Whatever you need, Joseph Wilkes will comply. Wilco.

No exceptions, other than Godfrey's stupid essay. But then that's not entirely my fault. It's mostly Eddie Olsen's fault. In fact, you could probably argue that it's entirely

Eddie Olsen's fault, because it was Eddie who sat with me in the library when I was meant to be proofreading the essay before handing it over to Godfrey, and who hit the 'find' button for Hitler. It was also Eddie who hit the 'replace all' button that turned Hitler into Titler. And we laughed about it, because for some reason it was hilarious to imagine what would happen if Godfrey actually handed in the essay like that. Plus, of course, boobs. But then the bell for form rang. And I forgot to hit undo before clicking save. It was only after I had handed the flash drive over and watched it being safely tucked into Godfrey's blazer pocket that I realised what I had done.

The three days between Godfrey handing in the essay and getting the mark back have been torture. The slight possibility that I did in fact undo the change became a recurring daydream. And how bad could it really be anyway? Those letters are all very close to each other on the keyboard, and maybe Godfrey could explain it away by freak sudden-onset dyslexia? Overall, it's likely that the teacher wouldn't really mind and would see the mistake for what it was: a harmless prank. The essay was a standard, suitably flawed B grade, and something silly like that would never stand between the Almighty Godders and the Gatford rugby team. Except that wasn't the point. Whether Godfrey could get away with it was never the point. I'd disrespected him. I had undermined him in front of his teachers and dared to make him look foolish. It

4

didn't matter what the consequences were, or whether there were actually any consequences at all. Nobody made Godfrey Chappell look stupid. Nobody would dare.

We had filed out of history innocuously enough – it was a standard unspoken rule to never start fighting in front of the teachers – but I could feel all their eyes on me, and could almost hear the fists clench and crack with readiness. A good fight was long overdue, and the boys were hungry for excitement. The moment I knew that I was out of the teacher's sightline, I darted, zipping through the mass of bottle-green blazers and fully aware that there were at least six boys on my tail. Their job was no doubt to catch me and pin me down so that Godfrey could do his worst. Or, if he was feeling particularly malevolent, he'd stand back, keeping his hands clean, while he told his henchmen what to do. I knew the drill. I jerked this way here, took an unexpected turn there, until I had managed to gain a substantial lead. Except that there was nowhere to go. Not really. All corridors eventually led to the central quad, and it was possible that if I could just reach that spot outside the staffroom, maybe the boys would leave me alone. But who was I kidding? Gatford doesn't have the kind of teachers who stand up strong in front of bullying behaviour. These teachers would sit by their window looking out across the central quad and watch the scuffle like a nature documentary: this was the natural order of things, and one mustn't interfere. Harmless rough-housing never did anyone any long-term harm, did it? Plus, it wasn't like any of the teachers would be on my side. I'm the scholarship kid. Of course there was going to be trouble wherever I went. It was to be expected. Nope, the staffroom wasn't an option.

So I ran out and through the quad, leaping with long strides out into the open, and then pushed straight through the double doors and into the west corridor. I heard the doors clang behind me as the gang pushed through, and then suddenly I saw the fire exit that led to the bins. The disgusting, smelly bins that none of those posh boys would go near if they could help it. At first I genuinely considered diving straight in, but then wouldn't I just be doing their job for them? Plus I would have to face the humiliation of clambering back out again, and then potentially have the smell lingering on me for the rest of the day, so I took a risk and aimed for *between* the dumpsters instead.

So here I am. It's cramped and, yes, the smell is putrid, but at least I can finally breathe again. Plus I have a vantage point to see the other boys speeding past. I quickly look up to the sky, hoping against hope that some flying Vigil will somehow hear my heart thumping and my lungs screaming and know that I'm in need of help. But no help comes. So I resign myself to waiting here until the end of lunch, when I can go to my next lesson, and hide within the relative safety of assigned seating. This will be fine. I just need to survive lunchtime without anyone spotting me.

The headache cracks through me like an electric bolt. I let my inhaler drop to the floor as I clutch at my temples and strain against the screwed-up contortion of my jaw. It's thirty seconds of pure agony. Like shrapnel pounding the inside of my skull. I manage to resist putting my weight against the dumpster, because if it moves then the boys might be alerted to my presence, so instead I press my forehead into the brick wall, willing the pressure to be soothing. It does nothing of course. The headache persists, and persists, until finally it dissipates. I see stars as my focus returns.

It's the second headache today, and the fifth this week. They're gaining in frequency, and intensity, and I wonder sometimes whether my brain might actually burst like a grape squished between fingertips if this goes on much longer. But now the pain has passed, it's as if it never happened at all. No change in vision, except for a final scattering of pinprick stars, and all fingers and toes apparently working perfectly – I've checked. I'm sweating, but that could easily be from the running. As far as I can tell, no damage done, not this time. But I'm not sure how many more of these I can take.

A loud *pop* breaks me from my worried self-assessment. I look out over the dumpster, and there are two girls standing there. One is using her tongue to snake tendrils of bubblegum back into her mouth, her arms folded tight across her chest, leaning heavily on one hip. The other is staring down at her feet, her heavy brown fringe practically hiding half of her face while girlish plaits hang down like curtains, her hands clasped tightly around the straps of her backpack.

'WILCO!' the first girl says. It's Maggie Monroe, Year 11 prefect and Gatford's most fearsome hockey player. She's always terrified me, not just because she's loud and bold (everything she says comes out of her mouth with exclamation points) but because if she knows who you are, it's probably because you're in trouble. She clucks on her gum as I stare back at her, the dumpster awkwardly positioned between us.

'Wilco! What the hell are you doing down there?' Maggie booms.

I go to make up an excuse, but it's soon clear that she's not expecting an answer.

'Where's that friend of yours, Eddie Olsen?' she continues. The girl with her doesn't even look up at me.

'Memorial garden, maybe,' I manage to stutter back.

'This is Kesia,' Maggie announces, head cocking to one side to indicate the shy girl next to her. 'She's new. She's into theatre. Eddie Olsen's into theatre too, right?'

I nod back at them as I emerge from behind the dumpster, acutely aware of how scruffy I must look. I'm

8

not sure why she's checking with me. Everyone knows that Eddie is Gatford's biggest theatre geek.

'Well, I need to be somewhere, so can you take Kesia over to see him and get him to tell her about the drama club?' It's not a question. It might sound like a question, but it's definitely not a question. And I'm Wilco, so no matter that a group of rampaging testosterone-driven boys are on the hunt for me, I will comply. I always comply.

'Sure ...' Maybe I can use Kesia as a human shield.

'Good. Cool beans. Kesia, this is Wilco. He'll look after you.' Then Maggie about-turns and marches off to whatever other important duty she has to do this lunchtime. Everything Maggie Monroe does is important.

Kesia doesn't look up at me, even when I say hello to her. Her eyes remain downcast, her arms tense like she's clinging on to her backpack for dear life. Right then. Should I be talking to her? Does she even want to be talked to? And what the hell is Eddie going to do with her once I take her over to him?

'You're new?' I try nervously.

I *think* she nods. But that could just be the way her head bobs as she walks, so I'm not sure.

'Have you been shown around?' I try again.

And again, another faint dip of the head that could be construed as an awkward nod. I guess that means she has been given the tour, but the memorial garden is at

9

least another three minutes away, and the thought of spending all that time with a girl and not saying anything makes the back of my neck sweat.

'That's the cage,' I say as we pass it, indicating the flat concrete desert of a playground surrounded on all sides by tall chicken-wire fencing. 'That's where the upper school play football during break.' I'm not entirely sure if she understands what I'm saying.

An old leather football suddenly flies towards us, and would have struck its target if it wasn't for the fencing. The clang of metal almost seems to ripple outwards, and somewhere within the cage someone yells, 'Sorry!' But I know the apology isn't for me.

'That was close!' But still she says nothing.

'That's the new block.' I nod towards the large modernist building, completely out of place next to the Victorian-gothic turrets of the old building. 'That's where humanities is, like English and history, and that big window is the library.'

Nothing from Kesia. Absolutely nothing. I don't even think she looks up. I wonder if she speaks any English. Her name sounds eastern European. Has she transferred from over there? Perhaps I should be speaking more slowly? I keep my head up and alert for interceptors the whole way; Godfrey's boys could emerge at any minute, and as much as I'd hope that Kesia would be an excellent human shield, I know I can't rely on it.

The memorial garden is just on the other side of the new block, a little rockery that sits under the lip of an upper storey. Even in the brightest sunshine it always seems to be in the shade. Eddie and I like it because the bench there stays dry in the rain.

Eddie doesn't see us approach. He's sitting on the bench, crouched over with hunched shoulders as he studies whatever novel he's reading this time. The garden is otherwise empty, thank goodness. Once in a while a shifty group of smokers will find their way over here and try to intimidate us into leaving, but at this time of year, and in this weather, most people are indoors looking for comfortable corners to relax in before the next round of lessons. Eddie keeps absently pushing a wavy strand of blond hair behind his ear, but it just flops forward again instantly. He's one of those people who always look like they could do with a haircut, even when they've only just had one.

'Eds,' I say. But then I have to say it again, louder this time, because Eddie's oblivious to anything that isn't words on a page.

When he does look up, his gaze goes instantly to Kesia, and his eyes widen in amazement, almost like he knows her and can't believe that she's here. Does he? Should I know her too? He pushes up his thick-rimmed glasses as he stands up; they have a habit of falling down his nose no matter how often they're tightened.

'This is Kesia,' I say, because he's not saying anything and it's starting to feel a little awkward. 'She's new. And Maggie wanted me to bring her over to you because of the theatre stuff.'

'You like theatre?' Eddie's voice rises at the end in an almost comical fashion.

I look at Kesia, to see how she's reacting, and her gaze remains unfocused and impassive. If Eddie knows or recognises her, it certainly doesn't appear to be mutual. Unless of course this is just how Kesia responds to everything, which I'm thinking now might be a plausible possibility.

'What do you like? Have you read Ibsen? I'm trying to make Ms Gibbs let us put on *Hedda Gabler*. Have you ever seen it?'

To this onslaught of questions, Kesia just tightens her grip on the straps of her backpack and lets her head cock slightly to one side.

'We're doing *The Crucible* in class, which is fine, but can be a little boring to stage, you know? Have you read *The Crucible*? Do you need any help catching up?'

Another slight head movement from Kesia, and Eddie's smiling like a goofy clown. I get the distinct impression that something is happening, and it suddenly dawns on me that Eddie doesn't know Kesia, he fancies her. I sit on the bench and take out my inhaler again for a top-up puff. Eddie continues yapping on to Kesia, who shuffles slightly on her turned-in toes.

12

'Hey, Eddie?' I interrupt. 'I need to tell you something.'

'Sure.' Eddie turns to look at me, but keeps glancing back to check that Kesia is still there next to him, as if she might magically disappear at any moment.

'Godfrey's after me.'

'He is? What is it this time?'

'Remember Titler?' I hiss.

'You didn't undo it?'

'Apparently not. His mates pounced on me after our lesson just now.' I pause. 'Hey, Eddie, you can get headaches from stress, right? I got this headache right after—'

'Get your eyes tested,' Eddie replies quickly, like he wants to be done talking with me, like he'd rather be talking to her instead.

'My eyes?'

'Yes. My cousin Felix – you know the one with all the music? He was getting headaches whenever he practised, and it turns out that he had an astigmatism. Meant that all the horizontal lines of music were messing with him. Plus, I always get headaches when my prescription changes.'

'I'm not sure it is that...' I try to think about whether my headaches have ever occurred when I was focusing on anything.

'Well, then... brain tumour?'

'What?'

'I mean, it's probably not a brain tumour. There'd be other symptoms. Probably.'

I take a moment to ponder this, and then wish I'd never brought it up.

'Oh man, Godfrey *does* look seriously pissed off!' Eddie exclaims suddenly.

I jump up from the bench, suddenly alert, and look over and see Godfrey and three of his friends approaching. This time there's nowhere to run. They're too close already, and I'm still feeling knackered from running away before. If I have to face Godfrey at some point, it might as well be now, with Eddie next to me and the presence of a girl to stop things getting too out of hand.

These boys might all be in Year Ten like me, but they all look like they're about twenty-five years old. All height and brawn and chest-space and jawlines, they stamp forward as a pack with Godfrey at the lead. He isn't even the biggest one. He isn't even the best-looking. And yet he has that indefinable thing that makes him the leader. That makes him king of the school. Maybe it's his ice-hard stare, maybe it's his fierce voice, or maybe it's because his father is some bigwig and more powerful than all the other fathers on the rugby team combined.

'Wilco!' Godfrey booms. 'Wilco, you prick!'

He's closer now, and I'm taking baby steps backwards to the bench, hoping and praying that a sinkhole will miraculously open up and swallow me.

Next to me, Eddie is tense; I can tell even without looking at him. Eddie is one of those kids the other kids leave alone, mostly because his parents are members of all the relevant clubs and societies, and Gatford pupils always seem to have an innate sense about who they can and can't get away with bullying. And he really doesn't like violence at all, even in the books he reads, and especially when that violence looks as if it's going to involve someone he knows. He reaches out a protective arm and grabs at me, as if somehow the physical contact might extend his protective bubble to me too, but Godfrey's now in spitting distance and edging even closer.

'Don't move!' Godfrey yells.

I should be running. I know this, and yet all I can do is screw my face up like I've just tasted something bad. I'm completely frozen to the spot as he approaches. It wouldn't take much for him to strike me. But he doesn't get a chance. Because just as he gets close enough, the edges of my vision start to disappear into smoky black, and I lose the feeling in my extremities. Has he already struck me without my realising? Has he secretly become proficient in beating people up psychically, without actually needing to make contact at all?

He looks about as confused as I feel, and for the briefest moment I get the sense that I must be doing something to frighten him, that something in the way I'm standing is wrong somehow. The ground seems to be rushing above me, and the sky plants itself firmly beneath my feet. When the headache cracks through my skull and wipes out the rest of my vision in one clean pounding, the last thing I see is Godfrey's face, mouth open wide in shocked panic.

2

'I didn't even do anything, did I? You saw me – I didn't do anything!' Godfrey is yelling.

When I open my eyes I find myself peering into the face of an angel. Her eyes gleam nearly gold under long lashes, and there's a curtain of dark hair framing her face. The sun behind her, just breaking through the clouds, looks like a halo, and all at once I'm overwhelmed, struggling to get my breath back, and feeling my heart racing in my chest. The angel's face is kind, gentle and worried, and she's so close that all it would take for my mouth to meet hers would be just the slightest of movements. Just a lift of the head, a reach forward, and . . .

'He's awake! It's OK, everyone! He's going to be all right!' The angel's voice is unexpectedly loud and piercing, and makes me wince as I try to work out what's going on.

I tip my head to avoid some glare and realise that my angel isn't alone. There are half a dozen more angels clustered around me, each with a halo backlit by the sun. Except, they're not angels. They are Godfrey and his minions, and over on the other side, peering over me like I'm an alien, are Eddie and Kesia. Eddie looks worried, and Kesia looks . . . well . . . it's hard to define her face as even having an expression. She's chewing on the end of one of her plaits, if that says anything at all. The chief angel, the one kneeling right over me, is in fact Indira Haynes, the most popular girl in our year and the girl I've been in love with for pretty much forever. She's quite possibly the most beautiful person I have ever known, and I can't imagine ever meeting anyone more perfect.

'Wilco, isn't it?' she asks me, one of her perfect hands cradling my head, the other on my shoulder.

She knows who I am! She knows my name! Except . . . that's not my name at all.

'Joseph, actually,' I manage to mumble back to her.

'Jeez, Wilco, mate, didn't realise you weren't well or anything,' Godfrey says, shifting awkwardly and running a hand back through his hair. I feel like pointing out that he is not, nor will he ever be, my *mate*, but my focus keeps shifting back to Indira, and the fact that she's *right here*. Next to me, with me, her hands actually touching me!

'I mean, we're all right, right? And you're all right, yeah?' Godfrey stutters.

I can't answer him straight away. Mostly because I have no idea if I am *all right*. The headache is gone . . . That's for certain. I wriggle my fingers and toes, checking I'm in one

18

piece. All there and accounted for... What the hell just happened?

'Seriously, Godders?' Indira asks Godfrey, her voice sharp.

'I did nothing! I swear!' he insists. His minions mutter and mumble around him.

'Well then, why is he on the ground like this?'

'He just fell over! Tell her, Wilco, you just spaced out and fell over! I wasn't anywhere near you!'

'I get these headaches sometimes...' I say, sounding like I'm questioning myself. 'And this one was the worst yet. I guess... I guess I must have blacked out?'

'But Godfrey was going to get him!' Eddie suddenly interjects. I'm a little surprised – Eddie would never normally get himself involved. Have I woken up in another universe? One where Indira touches me and Eddie butts in?

'I should take you to the nurse's room,' Indira says. Then, turning to Godfrey: 'Shame on you! We're going to talk about this later, OK?'

If Godfrey was a gorilla, he'd be puffing up and pounding on his chest right now, maybe stamping his feet in protest. But he's not a gorilla, so instead he bites the inside of his cheek and stuffs his hands in his pockets. He daren't argue with Indira, but the look on his face is clear: injustice streaked with rage.

'I swear I didn't touch him,' he protests again.

'But you came looking for a fight, didn't you?' Eddie says. Seriously, what has got into him?

'Whatever. He's clearly fine now. We're done here.' And with that, Commander Godfrey leads his troops back towards the main building and away.

I wonder if that means I'm off the hook, or whether he's going to look for a chance to punish me later on. In the grand social game of rock, paper, scissors, does faint trump fist?

'Can you stand up?' Indira helps me to a more comfortable, seated position, and once again her touch on my arm gives me an electric shock of hyper-reality. Indira Haynes. Right here, and right next to me.

She's being so utterly lovely and I'm wondering how she even got here. How long was I out cold for? Maybe that doesn't matter. What really matters is that she's here, and that I'm in her arms (not the ideal way around for these types of things, but whatever, I'll take what I can get) and her perfect eyes are focused entirely on me. She really is stunning. There's a rumour that her mum used to be a Bollywood film star back in India but gave it all up when she married Indira's dad and moved to the UK. And it's believable when you consider how beautiful Indira is.

'I feel OK now,' I stutter, fumbling a little as I get to my feet.

'But I really should take you to see the nurse. There might be something seriously wrong with you,' Indira says.

'No, really, I'll be fine. I'll make an appointment with the doctor when I get home later. But I'm sure it's nothing. People faint all the time, right?'

'It's his eyes,' says Eddie, pressing his lips together and nodding as if this is all old hat. 'He needs glasses.'

'Seriously, I'll be fine,' I insist.

Somehow her face manages to get even more beautiful when she looks concerned. I still can't quite believe that she's here, and that she's worried about me. This could definitely be the start of something. It has to be. This might be the very moment that she finally sees me. Not sees me in the regular sense, but really *sees* me.

'OK. But I have witnesses here who have seen me tell you to go to the nurse. I'm not going to be held responsible if you black out again.'

'Thanks, Indira, you're being really kind.'

'Well, just remember this when the voting opens for head girl at the end of the year. If you need anything, you come and find me, all right?'

I'm silent as she walks away and back into the main building. My mouth is dry and it's hard to swallow, but I don't think it's anything to do with the headache or the blackout.

'What was that all about?' Eddie demands, throwing both hands out dramatically.

'I did try and tell you about the headaches—' I start.

'Not your headaches, you idiot! Indira! You should have

21

gone with her! You need to milk this fainting thing for all it's worth!'

'But it's so embarrassing...'

'Are you kidding? Girls love it when they get to look after a guy! It's the whole maternal mothering instinct thing! Aren't I right, Kesia?' We both turn towards Kesia, who is back sitting on the bench. She offers no meaningful reply, just a shy tilt of her head. 'See! Kesia's on my side!'

'She was just being Indira. She's one of those people who cares about everyone, not specifically about me.' But even as I'm saying it, I'm hoping that I'm wrong.

'Indira Haynes. Wow, that's something.' Eddie turns to Kesia. 'Not that I care about girls in that way. I'm not about the outside; I'm all about what's on the inside. Real beauty lies within of course.'

I don't point out to Eddie that clearly Indira is a wonderful, selfless person on the inside too. As well as being one of the most responsible and sensible students in our year, destined to be head girl one day, she's also on the charities committee and ran a huge campaign last year to raise funds for sick children in Africa.

Rubbing my forehead, I'm wondering what to do next. It's nearly the end of lunch, and I suppose that technically I should take myself home, or ring Mum, or at the very least go to the nurse's room. Except that I feel absolutely fine. Better than fine in fact. I take a deep breath, expecting the usual constriction in my chest from the asthma. There's nothing, no resistance. My lungs and throat are completely clear.

'That was good work, you know, standing up to Godfrey. Thanks for that.' I want to point out that it was a very un-Eddie-like move, but then I twig that it was probably all for the purpose of impressing Kesia. His reply confirms my suspicions.

'You know, I would have punched him flat out myself if I had a chance to. Everything happened so quickly...'

'Yeah, well. Something tells me that this isn't over. Godfrey won't just leave things like that, will he? I bet he's going to make me pay at some point.'

'But not today! Today you got to lie in the arms of Indira Haynes!' Another quick look at Kesia. 'Not that Indira is anything special of course. But you know, she has quite a bit of sway in this place. Everybody loves her. Especially Joseph. He's been obsessed with her for ages!'

'Shut up, Eddie,' I say, wondering why Kesia isn't bothering to shut him up herself. Instead she just looks down at her shoes, as if neither of us was here at all.

My first lesson after lunch is English. And from the moment I enter the classroom I'm aware of Godfrey's mates sitting at the back. I swear I can feel their eyes on me, watching and judging, even when I'm not turning around to check. They still want a piece of me, I can tell.

Indira might have stopped me being beaten up for now, but it's definitely not over.

I'm jumpy. When I'm not thinking about the boys at the back of the class I'm thinking about Indira, and twice I have to nudge Rufus, who's sitting next to me, to point to where we are in the book we're reading, because I keep zoning out.

SLAM. Without my realising, my elbow has slid on the table and my head has plummeted down, my chin making a surprisingly loud noise as it makes awkward contact with the desk. I also manage to knock over my pencil case, sending it flying to the floor.

'Smooth move, Wilco!' someone bellows from the back. I don't bother turning round to see who.

Instead I manage to give a weak, apologetic wave to Mr Schuster, who is in the middle of some rant about how awesome *Jane Eyre* is, as I reach down to the floor to pick up my stuff. My favourite pen has rolled some way out to the side, so I have to lever myself out using my foot as a hook around the leg of my chair to keep stable. I really don't want to get up and walk to pick up the pen – that would be too awkward and obvious – but if I can just reach my hand out an extra inch or two ... then I can just about manage to stretch and grab it ...

The pen flies into my hand.

I don't even register it at first, it happens so suddenly. But as I straighten myself back up in my seat I really think about it. The pen was just out of reach, and then it wasn't. One moment it's out there on the floor, and then it's in my hand. I could have sworn that it moved by itself. But that's impossible, right? I look at the pen more closely. Could one of Godfrey's lot have replaced my usual pen with some sort of crazy trick kind? But no, that can't be right. This is quite clearly just a very ordinary pen.

'Something the matter, Mr Wilkes?' Mr Schuster asks. 'Or perhaps you'd like to contribute something on the theme of doubleness?'

'No, sir,' I mumble, putting the pen safely away in my pocket and deciding not to think anything more of it. I must have been mistaken. It couldn't have been as far away as I thought it was.

'Then I suggest that you pay attention to what some of the others are saying. You never know what might come up in your exams.'

Except that I find English so boring. Not the books, but the lessons. The books are all right, mostly. If only I could just read the books, and then not have to think about them. I don't care about themes, meaning or context. I just want to read whatever I am reading and then move swiftly on to the next thing. All this overthinking just makes me resent the book. It makes me resent all books.

I slink down in my seat and attempt to make myself as inconspicuous as possible. Surely if Mr Schuster can't see me, then he can't ask me any questions?

Once again thoughts of Indira creep into my mind, about what it would be like if we ever had a real conversation, just the two of us, alone. About where I'd take her if we ever went on a date together.

My gaze happens to fall on the bookshelves behind Mr Schuster's desk. I'm not really looking at them, it's just that's where my eyes happen to be focused as I daydream. One whole shelf is filled with battered copies of *Othello*. Mr Schuster has already warned us that it's what we're going to be studying next term. Can't wait for that. One of the books on the shelf – and only one – is placed upside down, ruining an otherwise perfect line of book spines, and even though I don't mean to, I find myself fixating on it. As Mr Schuster drones on about the significance of the colour red in *Jane Eyre*, I stare, imagining the book hovering off the shelf and righting itself in line with the rest.

And then the book falls.

Not just that one book, but all the books. A whole shelf of *Othello*s, plus some *Crucible*s from the shelf above and some *To Kill a Mockingbird*s from the shelf below, all tumble down to the ground in one clattering cascade.

Mr Schuster startles and clutches his chest at the sudden noise, and the boys at the back all spring to their feet to get a better look. I don't move. I can't move. I'm too scared. It's as if a ghost has rocked the entire shelving unit, or maybe it was a mini-earthquake? It has to be something like that. Something rational, if totally unlikely, because books don't just randomly fall to the floor for no reason. Not ones that I've been obsessive-compulsively staring at anyway. An earthquake isn't out of the question, or, if not that, maybe someone somewhere slammed a door, causing the whole building to shake? Maybe those shelves are placed at an awkward structural point? Maybe it was an accident waiting to happen?

So many possibilities. But there's also one more. One that I can't bear to consider. The pen, and then the books. *No, don't be ludicrous.* I almost laugh just from thinking that it might be a possibility.

When the end-of-lesson bell rings, Mr Schuster volunteers a couple of the girls from the front of the class to stay behind and put all the books back. He says he'll write them a note if they're late for their next lessons. When I walk past I feel guilty for not helping, as if somehow the books falling is my fault. But it wasn't my fault. How could it have been? In the corridors some of the kids talk about the weirdness of the incident, but it's soon forgotten. It was only a load of books anyway. A not even vaguely interesting detail in an otherwise normal day. Except for me. Because my fingers keep twitching with worry, I'm sweating at the back of my neck again and I can't help but wonder what would have happened if I'd have been focusing my energy on something else instead.

3

Getting out of school and down to the bus stop is a daily challenge. The first bus arrives approximately four minutes after the end-of-day bell, and if I can get out promptly I can run and catch it and escape the pain and brutality that is the second bus. Plus today there is the added pressure of avoiding Godfrey's gang.

I make it to the bus stop just as the first bus is departing. There are some Year Eights waving at me through the back window as it pulls away. I bend over, hands on knees, anticipating the inevitable rush of dizziness and breathlessness after that run down the hill from the school. I even automatically feel for my inhaler in my blazer pocket, all ready to remove it and puff for my life. But the breathlessness doesn't come. I stand up straight and test my breathing once again. Clear lungs, no wheezing. I don't even feel like I need to sit down. I'm at the front of the queue for the second bus and, relatively speaking, I feel pretty good. This is strange.

Is it possible to 'grow out' of asthma? Like how some people grow out of allergies or eczema? It must be possible, but to suddenly grow out of it in just one day seems unlikely. Maybe I'm just having a good spell. Maybe I'm being tricked into a false sense of security and will wake up in the middle of the night unable to breathe. And with my luck, it'll be when Mum is working a night shift too. I shudder when I think of being alone like that.

'Get out of the way, Wilco!' somebody calls as the second bus rounds the corner several minutes later, giving me a shove before I have a chance to complain.

After a beat I manage a disgruntled 'Hey!' but by this point my protest is useless.

To anybody looking, I'm now outside the queue, and in my place are three of Godfrey's best men. There are four Year Seven girls watching from just behind, their eyes wide with fear of the bigger boys, and in front of them I feel embarrassed. What can I do? Push back? No. That's not what I do. I can't. My pathetic 'hey' echoes around in my own head as the bus reaches the kerb and everyone ignores me. The rugby boys are kings of the school and they get on the bus without any hassle.

I courteously let the tiny Year Seven girls go in front of me. They don't say thank you. Then the queue goes crazy. A civilised line of schoolchildren turns into a scrum from hell as everybody clambers to get on the bus. They know that there's not enough room for all of them, and survival will rely on who can push and shove the hardest. I'm helpless as kids younger than me mimic the rugby boys and physically push me out their way, while others just shove their shoulders forward so that they can get ahead of the person next to them.

There's no way that I can compete. I've been here before, and my muscles can remember the bruises, so I know that the best tactic in this game is to wait for the third bus, with all the other loser kids. On the top deck one of the rugby boys has decided to moon those who are left on the pavement below, and I clench my jaw in frustration as I am forced to turn away. The rest of the kids laugh, of course they do. Of course it's hilarious that an upper-school boy has his cheeks out in a public place. But I don't find it funny. It's not funny that these kids get to do whatever they want, no matter who it might hurt. I don't find it funny that the owner of those cheeks will probably get lousy grades yet still end up running a multinational company one day. And what will I be doing? No doubt I'll end up like Mum, taking two jobs to make enough money to rent a poxy flat, never being able to afford my own place, laden with debt after taking a degree at a second-rate small-town uni.

As the bus pulls away I once again find myself at the front of the queue, the only upper-school kid left behind.

* * *

Mum is out at work when I get home, and I know that she won't be back until much later, so I busy myself by tidying the flat a bit and then get on with my homework. Mum works part-time late shifts at the big twenty-four-hour supermarket just outside town, alongside doing a regular day job as an office administrator for a firm of solicitors. We live above a newsagent's on a small parade of shops, where the vent for the kebab place next door comes out right next to our living-room window, making the air practically toxic. Mum will only have the windows open in the flat in the mornings, when the kebab shop is closed. Even in the hottest, muggiest summer months, those windows stay shut, otherwise the whole place ends up smelling of unidentifiable processed meat and stale grease.

The flat's bigger than the place we used to live in after we first moved out from Dad's (I had the one bedroom, and Mum slept on a foldout in the living room), but there's still not enough room. It isn't that Mum's a hoarder, at least not one of those really intense kinds where you end up not being able to see the carpet through all the junk, but she really doesn't like to throw things away. There are boxes loaded with magazines from her youth that she just can't bear to part with and crates stuffed with ancient shoes and bags that she hopes might come back into fashion one day. I've learned how to be frugal with my personal space and only cling on to the things that are absolutely necessary: my one-eyed blue teddy bear that I got when I was born (otherwise known as Mr Slim), a handful of toy cars given to me by a distant relative who died soon after and a box of CDs that my dad gave to me from when he actually took an interest and thought I might like to learn about his kind of music. (It's worth pointing out that he never gave me anything to play them on.) The less said about him though, the better. But despite my distinct lack of stuff, everything still feels too cramped here. One day I'll live in a proper house. One with two storeys. You wouldn't believe the number of times I've fallen asleep dreaming about owning a staircase.

I'm making lasagne when Mum finally gets home. I don't like eating this late, but it's worth it so that we can spend some time together. Plus I know that if I don't make something proper, she'll just have some cereal before crashing out in front of the TV.

'Quick! Turn the telly on!' Mum says, coming through the front door just after nine with a few bags of shopping, still wearing her supermarket tabard and name badge.

'Why? What's the emergency?' I ask.

'Debs let me off early so that I could get home in time. They've got that new Vigil girl on the Justin Moss Show! The one with the fire! They're interviewing her right now! Quick!'

She collapses on the sofa and I go to finish sorting the dinner.

'You are so sweet, you know?' Mum remarks. 'But sit down with me. Let's just watch this for a bit. Remember how much you used to love the Vigils? And that Deep Blue costume I made you for that birthday party? Is Deep Blue still your favourite?'

I don't tell her that I gave up on the Vigils a long time ago. I used to be obsessed with the escapades of the world's most famous international superhero team, but they never saved us from Dad, and once we got away from him and real life got shoved in my face, following their antics just seemed a bit of a waste of time. Plus I had much more important things to think about, like how to make spaghetti Bolognese for myself when Mum was working a double shift, or which neighbours were safe to turn to if I ever forgot my house keys and needed somewhere to crash until Mum got home. But I turn the Justin Moss show up loud anyway, because regardless of what we're watching, spending time together is rare and nice. Especially after the crazy day I've had.

'And later on tonight's show, I'm delighted that we're being joined by the Vigil's newest rising star – the girl is so hot right now, let me tell you – the wonderful Vega will be joining us live in the studio!'

Mum does a little squeal and claps her hands at the telly. I cross my arms and try to stifle a yawn.

After a stilted interview with a second-rate movie star who clearly does not want to be there, the new Vigil girl they are calling Vega makes her entrance.

The first thing that strikes me is how young she is. It's hard to tell behind her mask, but I figure that she can't be more than eighteen. She has a certain bounce in her step that makes her seem younger than any of the other superheroes I've seen, energetic and sparkling. She's in full costume, a black catsuit with boots that seem to glimmer molten red under the studio lighting. A simple, burglar-type mask obscures most of the top half of her face, but she's smiling brightly, showing off all her perfect teeth, and has hair that reminds me of Indira's, in that it looks like supermodel shampoo-advert hair.

'So, Vega, you're from the UK, but you've been away for a while, haven't you?' Justin asks her.

'I was stationed in New York for most of my special training, yes. It was good to get away and be somewhere new – it definitely helped me focus – but now I'm back in my home country and I can't wait to get to work as a full-time member of the London team,' Vega replies.

'You'll be a new face to a lot of the viewers out there; nobody's had a chance to really see you in action yet. Can you tell us a bit about what you can do?'

'Well, Justin, I can do this...' Vega holds out a hand and the camera zooms in close. She rubs her thumb and forefingers together, as if rolling an invisible ball. And then a tiny flame appears. It flickers, tentative and tiny, until she opens out her hand wider and the flame is bold and bright. Her entire right hand is aflame.

34

I'm pretty impressed. I wasn't planning to be, but I am despite myself. Pyro-kinesis is pretty damn cool.

'But that's not all you can do, is it?' Justin Moss teases. 'We've set up some equipment on the other side of the studio, if you'd like to show us?'

Vega obliges with a beaming grin. The TV people have set up a scarecrow – a really ugly-looking thing made out of sticks, straw and rags – and Vega stands about eight feet away from it. The camera catches sight of some studio assistants trying to keep out of shot, all brandishing fire extinguishers. Without any hesitation, and with every part of her radiating pride, Vega holds both her hands out towards the scarecrow. In seconds it's alight, and like a conductor manipulating an orchestra, she makes the flames burn brighter and then dimmer with a graceful flourish of her arms. The studio audience breaks out into rapturous applause (Mum starts clapping too), and after Vega extinguishes the flames with one last elegant gesture, she goes back to join Justin Moss on the sofa, pleased as pie.

'No trickery there, folks – our budget won't stretch that far! That was brilliant! Wasn't it incredible, ladies and gentlemen?' Justin gives Vega her own mini standing ovation as she settles back down next to him. 'So tell us a bit more about yourself. Other than setting fire to things, what's Vega really about?'

'Oh, Justin, you know I can't give you too many details. What I can say is that up until about a year ago, I was just another normal schoolgirl. I had no idea about what was happening to me.'

'What was it like then, suddenly discovering that you had superpowers?'

'Well, for starters there was nothing *sudden* about it. It was a slow, painful transition. There were signs that perhaps I could have recognised earlier, but so much of it was so similar to what any teenager goes through, I didn't think any more of it at the time.'

'What kind of signs?'

'I understand that it's a little different for everyone, but for me it was hot flushes. Excruciating hot flushes. And sweating, which was *lovely*, and then the dreams. The dreams were pretty telling actually. I should have paid a lot more attention to them sooner.'

'And were you alone through all of this? How did you cope?'

'I wouldn't have survived any of this without my best friend. And no, I'm not going to give you any more details than that. Their privacy and security is of utmost importance to me, as you can imagine. But what I would say to anyone who thinks they might be going through a similar change, is to find out early who you can trust, and never give up hope on them. Whether they are a family member or a friend, try not to do it alone. You're going to need people you can trust and love around you for the whole journey.'

Justin nods and asks her some more questions about her new life, probing for details about the Vigils' London base, which she dodges like a pro. By this point I'm only half listening. Because I'm thinking. Thinking about what happened in class earlier, and what it might mean.

Finally, hiding his frustration at having unearthed no secrets about the Vigils, Justin wraps up the interview. 'Vega, it's been an absolute pleasure to have you on the show – hasn't it, ladies and gentlemen? Join me in welcoming a bright new star to the constellation of London Vigils!'

The audience goes crazy for her, and even Justin Moss seems to be approving. I look over at Mum, and can see that she's crazy for her too. Mum loves the Vigils. She claims to have only a passing interest, but I know the truth: that on her lunch and coffee breaks she reads all the gossip magazines, catches up on all the websites. She follows their exploits and scandals like a soap opera. It must be a nice distraction.

We unpack the shopping once the Justin Moss Show is over (the less said about the tub of ice cream that wasn't put straight in the freezer, the better) and eat a bit of the lasagne. Mum's tired though, and can't eat much now that it's so late. She yawns while giving me a hug, and then makes for her bedroom.

'You should go to bed too,' she says.

'I'm not quite ready yet. I'm going to watch the news,' I reply. I've never had a set bedtime, not since I was tiny anyway, and Mum has always trusted me to look after myself. Being a latch-key kid from such a young age has its advantages.

I turn the sound down on the television so that it doesn't bother Mum – the walls in our flat are thin. I don't actually know what I'm going to watch. We don't get any of the fancy channels, just the regular Freeview stuff, and I have a bad habit of not keeping track of whatever it is everybody else is into watching. I flick through the channels once, and then again, before I settle on the nightly news programme on BBC2. I'm not remotely tired yet, so I'm hoping that I might be able to bore myself to sleep.

The man on the telly is serious, sitting forward in his chair, his tie uncomfortably tight around his collar. There's something I recognise about him, something in the way he purses his lips and squints at the man he's arguing with. They're talking about the Vigils, I think, so this might be at least partly interesting. I put the remote control down next to me and settle back in the sofa.

'So whom do the Vigils serve? Are you saying that they should only be rescuing people who can afford to pay for it?' the host of the programme asks.

'No, that's not what I'm saying,' the serious man replies. 'As chairman of the Vigil Select Committee, I have a parliamentary responsibility to make sure that the system stays fair for everyone. But in these times of austerity, cuts have to be made, and the government can't afford to keep everything public. It's the same with our hospitals, and with our schools.'

'What if there were a public emergency? What if there were a terror attack?'

'Now, Hugh, I think it's safe to say here that since the Vigils have come under government jurisdiction as an adjunct to the Ministry of Defence, there has been a marked decrease in terror attacks and suchlike. It simply is not a feasible target for these terrorists, once they know that there are publicly funded people in masks flying about. And it's like with our health service: when it comes to emergency care, the British have the best health system in the world. Likewise, with the Vigils, we have one of the best-funded teams in the West, outside of the United States. In a time of emergency, every single man, woman and child has access to the best in public safety and protection.'

'So then, let's talk about the Ditko Finance building fire. There are claims of back-office deals and insurance scams, people are saying there was evidence that you had been overseeing dodgy deals that benefited Ditko and taking a cut. There are some who would speculate that it was all very convenient for you, that you personally had a lot to gain from the destruction of evidence in that very office. Is it a coincidence that your office held back the authorisation for the Vigils to go in and make the building safe? Were they waiting for the go-ahead from you, which was only granted once you knew the key evidence would have been destroyed? Need I remind you that two people died in that fire? With a further three sustaining life-changing injuries and burns. If the Vigils had been allowed to do their job unhindered by your office, would those people be alive and well now? Is Vigil protection for sale, Mr Chappell?'

Chappell! I knew I recognised his face! That's Godfrey's dad, right there on the television. And now that I know it's him, I realise that the family resemblance is uncanny. I knew that he was big in politics, but for some reason the fact that he is chair of the Vigil whatnot committee had completely passed me by. Now that I think about it, that's probably how Godfrey ended up with a birthday card from Quantum last year. He brought it into school with him but wouldn't let anybody else touch it.

'Firstly, I've made very clear that although I do have historic dealings with Ditko Finance, I have had very little to do with them over the last decade. Secondly, it was an unfortunate turn of events that prevented Vigil teams from accessing the site, and lastly, let's make sure that our focus is drawn back to remembering those who died and were injured in the fire. This was a massive human tragedy, and I don't think it serves anyone to start rewriting history in order to validate your elaborate conspiracy theories.'

'But, Mr Chappell, you haven't answered my question. How much did Ditko Finance pay to have you look away while their building conveniently burned?'

'Accusations of "paid saves" or "paid protection" have been dogging the Vigils since their emergence and ratification back in the fifties and sixties. What you are ignoring is the great human tragedy, and the rational acceptance that tragedies do in fact happen, even in our super-powered world, whether we like it or not.'

'Answer the question, Mr Chappell. Have you personally gained from dealings with Ditko Finance in the wake of the fire?'

'There is no question to answer here. The supposition that I might have had anything to do with this tragedy, or that I ever could have possibly financially gained from it, is entirely preposterous.'

'Douglas Chappell, MP and chair of the government's Vigil Select Committee, thank you for your time.'

I turn the telly off and stare at the blank screen for a little bit, the electronic hum lingering in my ears for a while longer. Most of the time I let all the Vigil stuff pass me by, but after seeing Vega earlier it feels strange for them to be involved in a more negative story. I guess I always thought that they were the most uncontroversial people in the world. After all, they save people and protect things! I'm not sure I like the idea of government bigwigs having control over them and potentially using them for their own profit and gain. It's like playing chess with actual people.

Tiredness finally catches up with me. By the time I'm in bed I'm back to thinking about Vega, and about how lucky she is. Her life must be perfect now, with access to whatever she wants, the parties and the fame. To be one of them, one of the Vigils, would solve all of my problems, that's for sure. Mum and I could live somewhere that doesn't come with kebab-stink, Godfrey would leave me alone, and surely there wouldn't be so much pressure from the scholarship conditions? Maybe girls like Indira would finally start to notice me, properly this time, and not just because I fainted.

In the quiet of my bedroom I stare up into my light bulb, not caring about the retina burn.

Then a strange thought comes. A thought that I'm only entertaining because I'm alone, and nobody can see me. I turn my head so that I'm looking at my bedroom door, towards the light switch. And then I focus. I focus so hard that my jaw hurts from clenching and my eyes water, but I never lose my intention. I don't let go. I see the light switch in front of me, and I can see it again in my head. I reach out for it with my mind . . .

The light goes out.

4

I wake up the next morning with my heart thumping, which isn't altogether comfortable to be honest. I wonder if I'm having a heart attack. I wonder if I'm going to be one of those perfectly healthy kids who suddenly drops down dead because of an undiagnosed heart condition. It wouldn't be that unusual – when I was in Year Seven it happened to one of the upper-school boys on the rugby team. One minute in a scrum, the next lying dead in the mud. Then the realisation dawns on me: my heart isn't racing because I'm ill, but because I'm excited. I'm going to be a superhero. My breathing hitches as I remember what happened yesterday, and the drumming in my chest pounds even louder. I remember when I was younger how I felt when I woke up on Christmas morning, and even though I always knew I wasn't going to get the most expensive presents, this is just like that. It's the thrill of the mystery, when you know that the outcome will only ever be good. Today is the first day of the rest of my life. From now on every minute will be like Christmas, because I get to be one of them, a Vigil. Holy cow, I'm going to be a superhero!

When I try to move I realise how tired I am. Not just first-thing-in-the-morning tired, but mega just-run-up-six-flights-of-stairs tired. I think it's because of the dream I had in the night. In the dream I was with them – Quantum and Deep Blue and Vega – and I could control stuff with my mind. I could make clouds move, I could make leaves blow off trees, and I think I even managed to topple a car over. There's another heart flutter as I think about everything I might be able to do now.

Except, was it all just a dream? What if my imagination got a little carried away? I mean, moving on from books, pens and light switches to flipping cars? And that's presuming that it was in fact me controlling that stuff. Surely it can all be rationally explained somehow.

I need to test it again. I need to make sure.

Sitting up on the crazed mess that is my bed (somehow I've managed to kick off my duvet and sheets during the course of the night), my blinds still closed and the rest of the world a million miles away, I stare at my teddy bear, Mr Slim. He usually sleeps on the bed with me – I'm not one of those babyish kids who has to have a teddy bear with him when he sleeps, it's just that this is where he always is – but he's fallen to the floor. It's early, and my muscles may be tired, but I'm buzzing with an energy that usually only ever comes after a gallon of fizzy drinks. I sit on my hands to make sure that I'm not tempted to use them, and I focus. I focus hard.

At first nothing happens. It's frustrating, but I figure that there must be some special switch in my head, and all I need to do is tap into it. Focus...Focus...There it is! It's actually easier with my eyes closed, because I can envision Mr Slim in my mind's eye much more easily. I can feel the fuzziness, and the strange cuddly warmth of him. I levitate Mr Slim up, and open one eye, then the other. It takes a lot of concentration, but as long as I can hold my breath, I can hold him. Eventually I have to breathe out though, and when I do, he drops sharply back down to the floor.

Wow, my body aches; it's mental! There's a tension between my shoulder blades that's making my arms feel heavy, and an echo of a headache just at the back of my skull. Not like the bone-splitting pain I've been getting, but something duller and more persistent. It makes me want to flop back in bed and sleep for a century. I wonder if the brain responds to a workout the same as the body does: maybe this is like muscle soreness after a particularly taxing PE lesson, except for my brain.

I finally manage to pull myself up and out of bed when I hear Mum turn the shower tap off in the bathroom. This is usually my cue to use the bathroom, otherwise Mum'll knock on my door to check if I'm up, and I hate it when she does that. I groan as I reach for my bedroom door, and practically crash into Mum on the landing. (Our flat is so tiny that crashing into each other is not exactly a rare event.)

'Morning, sunshine!' she says. 'You all right?'

'Yeah, just about,' I say.

Do I tell her? Do I tell her everything? No, she'll only worry, and more than anything I don't want Mum to worry. I can't tell her about any of this, not until I'm better at it. And not until I stop feeling like I've been hit by a speeding train...

I linger in the shower, feeling the water stream over my upturned palms. As the droplets sparkle and fly around me, I try to imagine being able to control them. At first I think I have it. As I see the water in my head, it's like I can move it as one stream, like rerouting the meander of a river. But I lose it quickly – you can't hold water as a stream. Too quickly it breaks down into droplets, and then micro-droplets, and then the focus is gone. There's a painful twist in my temples as I try again, signalling that maybe I should just focus on getting myself clean and ready for school. Damn it, I hope that the pain in my head and the soreness will wear off at some point. What's the point of these powers if it's going to be so uncomfortable all the time? Maybe this is how it starts for everybody? I mean, can you imagine how Deep Blue's head must have felt as his mind grew and adapted and mutated into what it is today? And on the telly last night, didn't Vega say that she had had a 'painful transition'? Hopefully that's all this is. I just have to wait it out and push through, and *then* I'll be the true superhero I'm meant to be.

'Are you sure that you're all right?' Mum asks me over toast and cornflakes.

I'm nearly too excited to eat, but Mum has a whole thing about breakfast and how important it is, so I don't want her to get even more concerned. I swirl the flakes around in my bowl with my spoon, before forcing myself to slurp them up.

'Definitely,' I reply. 'Just a bit worried about a test.'

'What subject?'

'Maths,' I lie.

'Your father was good at maths. Which is just another sign that you're more my son and not his. The only reason I can do the checkout at work is that it's all calculated for you. I don't know how they used to manage without the computerised tills.'

'I'll need a good grade for sixth form,' I say.

'Of course you do. And you'll study hard, like always. You'll do fine, I just know it.' And then, after a beat, 'There's nothing else bothering you? I heard you tossing and turning in the night.'

Damn our thin walls.

'Can't even remember what I was dreaming about...' Another lie. I don't want to get into this habit, but it's so much easier than telling the truth.

47

'Teenage boys,' Mum mutters to herself before getting up to make another cup of coffee.

I look down at the cornflakes in my bowl, and while her back is turned I screw up my face and focus hard. The soggy flakes float over to one side and then the other, as if my mind is a moon turning the tide. It's amazing. I mean, it's small, but it's amazing, and already I feel like I'm getting better at it. I think about the dream, about lifting the trees and flipping the cars, and then think about all the other things I'm going to be able to do with my powers. I think about how impressed everybody will be. About how Godfrey will never bother me again, and how girls will flock to my side, desperate for my company. And not just any girls either. Indira. She'd have to notice me, especially if I'm flying over the rooftops of Gatford with her in my arms!

I'm late for my usual bus by the time I manage to leave the house, but for the first time in a long while I don't care. I prefer to get the earliest bus I can to school, because frankly it's quieter, calmer and less likely to be filled with kids who hate me, but today walking to the bus stop is a slow slog, punctuated by me needing to have the odd breather on a neighbour's front wall. The asthma might not be there – my lungs are clear and easy – but this is something else entirely, and just as painful.

The bus is packed with Gatford kids. I can't believe that there once was a time when all I wanted in life was to be one of these students. I'll never forget the first time I saw the Gatford House uniform: I was out with Mum, and I saw a group of them outside a coffee shop. The boys were all tall and broad-shouldered, with shiny black shoes and expertly arranged ties. The girls all wore dark socks pulled up to their knees, and one even had a ribbon in her long blonde hair. They looked like the kind of schoolkids I read about in old adventure books, who drank ginger ale and solved mysteries in their half-term holidays.

'What school do they go to?' I remember asking Mum.

'Gatford House. It's on the other side of town.'

'Can I go there?'

'I don't think so, Joseph. You have to pay lots of money to go there. The Academy is free.'

But the Academy was where everyone else in my primary-school class was going, and the thought of spending the next seven years of my education with them filled me with dread. I wanted to be different from them, I wanted to be special – like the kids in the dark green uniforms.

From the moment I first saw them, I was enthralled. I always thought that was where I was meant to be, that somehow my life would make sense if only I could get there. The scholarship wasn't easy to come by either. I had to fight for it. There were cleverer kids than me in my primary school, but I worked the hardest. Why I thought that the hard work would end after I got accepted, I don't know. If anything, it just got harder, for me and for Mum. Attendance at Gatford House might be free on the scholarship, but there are countless other things that need to be paid for. Like the uniform, and the books. And even with Mum holding down two jobs, there's still no way that I can go on all the expensive trips, like skiing, or to the theatre with Eddie.

I have to admit, as much as I've come to dread the place, the approach to the school is pretty stunning. You can just about see the main building from the road, especially at this time of year when the trees are nothing but wispy skeletons, and the budding leaves mean that each branch and twig has its own aura of translucent green. Beyond the long driveway, the building itself is a rambling monstrosity (some say that it used to be a lunatic asylum), with long corridors and high ceilings hidden behind a dark redbrick facade. In some places it reminds me of a church, complete with gabled windows and gargoyles for gutters, and sometimes it seems more like an ancient country manor house that should have fallen and crumbled by now, if it wasn't for the money of the pupils' parents. Thankfully you can only see the main building from the approach. All the other buildings, like the sports hall and the modernist humanities building, are hidden behind like architectural parasites.

Of course, when I first saw the entrance I thought my

education was going to be one long gothic adventure with capers and ghosts around every corner. I thought that Gatford was made for me. I never once suspected that I might not be made for Gatford. Mum doesn't know how I feel. After all the work she does, if she knew how unhappy I've become here then it would break her heart. That's why I have to make all this work. I have to make it worth it, for the both of us.

As I push myself through the school gates and up the long drive, I have to remind myself what Mum always says to me whenever I'm feeling down about our place in the world: that I'm playing the long game. That going to Gatford House brings along with it opportunities that I would never have had otherwise, and that maybe one day, if I just work hard enough, I might get to be on the same level as the other kids here. It's the only way to make this walk each morning not feel like I'm dragging myself through sludge.

Except…what happens now? If I'm going to be a superhero, does any of this matter?

Eddie is already in the memorial garden, hunched over a book. I sit next to him on the bench, and when he doesn't say anything to me, I reach down and under to see what it is he's reading. It's a collection of Shakespearean sonnets.

'I thought you were studying Keats?' I ask, because why would anyone read poetry when they don't have to?

'I'm looking for something...' Eddie says, not lifting his gaze from the page.

'Well, good morning to you too...' I want him to see me, to realise that something has changed, as it will make the whole breaking-my-news-to-him thing much easier.

He starts mumbling a passage aloud. Something about a woman's face, painted hands and gentle hearts. I think about how he was with Kesia, and decide that I don't like where this is going at all.

'Do you think that it's too much?' he asks, looking at me with such earnestness in his eyes that it makes me squirm.

'For what exactly?'

'For Kesia!'

'Mate...a love poem? Wasn't Valentine's day last month?'

'But Kesia wasn't here last month. And I want to be romantic and chivalrous and gentlemanly!'

'Has she even spoken to you yet?'

'Yes! Well...OK, not exactly. She's not the most vocal of people in the world. But she's shy! And she just needs to get to know me!'

'You don't think that a love poem by Shakespeare might scare her off?' I might have exactly the same experience with girls as Eddie (which is precisely none), but I also think my instinct on this is better than his.

'Well...but...isn't this how it used to be done?'

'Deeds, not words,' I advise, as if I have all the answers. I think about Indira, and how one day (maybe very soon!) I'm going to show her exactly what I'm capable of. I won't have to say a thing, and she'll see why she should be with me.

'Are you OK?' Eddie says suddenly, looking up from the book and pushing his glasses up on his nose.

'Yeah . . . why?'

'You seem . . . weird. More so than usual, that is.'

'Well, here's the thing . . .' I start, thinking that this is it, this is the perfect moment to tell him absolutely everything. 'There's something I need to tell you, and it's kind of strange but you have to listen, OK?'

'OK . . . ?'

I take a deep breath, realising that this is a huge moment, not just for me, but for Eddie too. Is he prepared to be my confidant? Just because he's the only person I can talk to, does that mean that he's the best?

'Kesia!' Eddie cries.

She emerges from around the side of the building, hands crossed over her chest and eyes half-hidden by her fringe, wandering slowly, as if she's nervous to approach. I sigh, maybe a bit too audibly to be polite. She doesn't seem to notice, but then again I'm not entirely sure if she notices anything.

Eddie quickly shoves the book of sonnets in his bag, then jumps up to say hello. He starts telling her about

53

something else he's reading, and asking if she's read it too. It's strange, how he can have a complete conversation with someone despite the fact that he's the only one talking.

'Oh, Joseph, what was it you were saying?' Eddie says eventually, turning back to me.

As if on cue, the bell for first registration starts to sound.

'Nothing important,' I sigh, because now is clearly not the time to be having the conversation that I want to have. Not when bells are ringing and Eddie's thoughts are obsessed with a girl.

I'll try again later, or maybe tomorrow, some time and place where I know there aren't going to be any interruptions.

'You sure, mate?'

'Definitely, don't worry about it,' and we start to head off to registration, as if everything is perfectly normal. As if *I'm* still perfectly normal.

I try again the next day, and the next, but the timing is never right. I just can't get Eddie on his own. Every time – every single time – Kesia is right there. She meets with us for lunch, and if she's not in Eddie's classes, then she's in mine. Always nearby, never saying anything. It doesn't feel like she's my friend, even though she's around so much. She feels like something I want to shake off, like tissue paper stuck to the bottom of my shoe. But it's hard to be actually annoyed with her, because she doesn't do anything that's particularly annoying. Nothing that I can put my finger on anyway. She's quiet, moves like a mouse, and hardly ever says a word if she can help it. Eddie is clearly, pathetically smitten, but doesn't seem to notice how cool she is in response. Just the fact that she's there – always there – seems to be enough to spur him on. He's so happy to have her there, and I wonder, if the situation was different and it was Indira hanging around us all the time, whether I wouldn't be behaving in exactly the same way. I also wonder, if I didn't have this immensely momentous thing going on in my life, whether I would even care. But still. He must be noticing how frustrated I've been getting, surely?

'Hey, buddy!' Eddie greets me as I come and sit down next to him in physics. Kesia's not here yet. She was in my last class, and I know that I probably should have waited and walked over with her, but I figured that this would be the last chance I would get today for a one-to-one with Eddie. So I rushed out and sped over here, because I know that our physics teacher is always a little late, and keeping this secret all bottled up is starting to feel like it's killing me.

'Eds, look, here's the thing...' I've got it all planned out. I know exactly what I'm going to say.

'Are you all right?'

'Yes, I'm fine, I'm better than fine, in fact. Look—'

But there's no time. She's here. How the hell did she manage to get here so fast? I practically ran the entire way, and I've never seen her move any quicker than Fat Henry. Kesia smiles when she sees us already at our desk, and I swear there's an expression of satisfaction on her face. What's her plan? Is she trying to come between us? But if there was a smirk there at all, it's gone now. Her shy eyes are downcast as she takes her books out, and she lets her hair fall forward across her face as she sits down.

'What is it then? Spit it out,' Eddie says to me.

'Nothing,' I murmur.

'Come on, you've been funny for ages now.' He leans in close and whispers, 'Is it about...?' He nods his head towards Kesia.

'No!' I startle. Then more quietly: 'It's not that at all. But we never seem to get any time for ourselves any more, do we?'

The teacher arrives and we stop talking. Eddie definitely knows that something is up, mainly because I'm finding it so difficult to hide my frustration. Does he think that I'm jealous of all the attention he's giving Kesia? Does he think that I don't like a girl coming between us? I guess he's right in a way. It's just, the more blundered attempts I make to talk to him, the more desperate I feel. And it's making me resent *her*, even though technically she has nothing to do with anything.

I placate myself by keeping my hands under the table, my pen hovering just above my fingers. As our teacher starts going on about the structure of the atom, I scowl and concentrate on the pen, on not letting it fall, so that I can try to stop feeling like a bubble that's about to burst.

5

It's been a week since I discovered that I have super-powers, I'm on the roof of the school and I'm about to jump.

No, things haven't got that bad; I'm just trying to work out whether or not I can fly. I need to know. I'm not on the edge of the roof, but actually perched on a little ledge that hangs down from the older part of the building over the science block. It's a drop of only a few feet, if that, but it gives me the chance to feel like I'm standing on a precipice, as if the threat of imminent danger might be all I need to encourage whatever is going on in my head to adapt just that little bit further. If all goes to plan, very soon I'll be swooping down over the science block and off over the lawn and the school fields beyond. Wouldn't that be something?

I decided that doing this in my school uniform wouldn't be the smartest of moves, so I've put my blazer and tie in my locker and I'm going for the covert look, with a black hoodie over my school shirt. The zip is done up the whole way (hiding the whiteness of the shirt) and the hood pulled up so that, from a distance, you can't tell that it's me. At least I hope not.

The world pans out in front of me, with Gatford House's vast sports fields merging into empty countryside that stretches right up to and beyond the horizon. It's been another crisp early-spring day, and the sky is still a brilliant blue despite the sun behind me already getting rather low. Long shadows crawl out from the buildings, and somewhere just out of sight the sound of the girls' hockey team doing their practice carries on the breeze.

So how exactly do I do this? Do I just let myself go and step off the ledge? Do I jump up first, or should I leap forward? I shift on my feet, as if waiting for the answer to become obvious, but it doesn't, and I'm left feeling really stupid. Why should I presume that I can fly? Just because I can move things with my mind doesn't mean I can suddenly leap tall buildings in a simple bound . . . But I have to try, because flying would be the ultimate. I imagine myself sitting in assembly, getting bored during one of the head's gargantuan speeches about the importance of manners and respect. In the daydream I stand up, having had enough, and every face turns to look at me. Pushing past the people in my row to get out of the hall would be an awkward nightmare, but I have a solution: I hover and rise, zooming up in the air and curling loop-the-loops, to everyone's amazement, before heading out and away, never to return. So long, suckers, I'm finally free!

That said, I'm still just standing here, on the ledge, and I'm getting a little bit cold now. I do a little half jump, nothing too enthusiastic, and feel a little depressed when gravity inevitably tugs me back down. I squeeze my eyes shut and clench my fists too, searching in my mind for that little internal switch that will suddenly reveal all the answers. But there's nothing there. Except...I can still see things. With my eyes closed. Like the dank football that looks like it's been lost up here on the roof for aeons, and a golf club that might have been left here from some old prank. At first I think that it's just my imagination working overtime, but it also feels more than that. I'm not sure, and when I try and push further it ends up making me dizzy.

Eyes open again, I look towards some of the gunk in a nearby gutter. It's all wet and cold and slimy. Then, just up a bit, there's a loose tile on the roof. The cold ceramic clatters and slinks further down the slope of the roof as I focus on it and use my mind to play with it, until finally it comes free and slides down on to the flat part of the roof where I'm standing. Next my attention turns to that old football, half deflated and sad-looking in the corner. I kick at it with my mind. It doesn't move much, but it leans slightly, as if about to tip into a new position. Was that me? Wow – I still can't quite believe that I can do this!

'Joseph!' The voice is far away, muffled by the breeze, so at first I'm not even sure I heard it.

The second time is loud and clear though: 'Joseph!' Eddie?

I see him standing on the field. There shouldn't be anyone out there at this time – that's why I picked today to try this out – but shouldn't Eddie be in after-school chess club? What the hell is he doing here?

'Don't do it!' he calls up to me.

'What?' I shout back.

'I said, DON'T DO IT!'

Does he . . . ? Does he think that I want to jump? I mean, I do want to jump, but not like that. I realise that from his viewpoint me standing here on the ledge can't look good.

I decide to try one more time, to see if this sudden flood of panic is enough to do it, to make me fly. I stand with my toes just over the ledge of the roof, with the next level within easy reach below me. I squeeze my eyes shut really tight, and I jump.

FLY! FLY! FLY! I'm telling myself as the world drops away, and then returns again with a painful thud.

It was a simple jump, not a dive, so I've pretty much landed on my feet, except that my feet weren't exactly ready to be landed on and have crumpled below me. I drop and roll on the flat roof, before looking up again and out on to the field. Eddie's not there. He must be coming for me. I let out one last long sigh and then go to clamber back on to the higher part of the ledge, which leads to the access door.

'What the hell was that?' We end up meeting not far from the lockers where I've left all my stuff.

'I can explain…' I start, not really sure where to start.

'I knew that something was up, and you've been strange all this past week – is this what you've been wanting to talk to me about? Surely… surely it's not this bad!'

'Eddie, I wasn't trying to jump off the roof. Well, I was actually, but not for the reason you think.'

'Joseph, seriously, are you OK?' He's got both his hands on my arms, gripping hard, almost like he wants to shake me.

'I'll tell you,' I reply. 'Something is happening, and it's weird. I've been trying to tell you for ages now. But not here. Can we go back to yours?'

Eddie looks at his watch. His sister's netball practice finishes in ten minutes. His mum will probably be waiting in her Range Rover outside the school. Guess there's no backing out now.

It could be so easy to hate someone like Eddie. His house has an attic *and* a cellar, his dad drives a BMW and his mum pays someone to do her nails, even when she's not going anywhere special. He's got so many siblings and they're all nice and seem to like each other, plus they go on two holidays a year – summer and winter. His parents read newspapers and there are actual paintings of ancient relatives on the walls, not just photos.

Eddie leads me up the gravel drive to his front door and my thoughts linger on the satisfying crunch of tiny stones under my feet. I don't think he realises that I always keep a few steps behind him. It's because I'm scared that some maid will turn me away. Not that the Olsens actually have a maid, but it's just what I imagine. I expect there to be someone waiting for me just inside, ready to tell me to go away because I'm not good enough. Even when I am inside, when we're just chilling out in his room, I can never fully relax. I worry about tracking mud in on my shoes, or my fingers being too dirty to touch anything.

Eddie's mum, who insists on me calling her *Jem*, not Mrs Olsen, drops us off in the driveway before pulling out again with Eddie's little sister Merry still in the car. Apparently she needs new dance shoes.

As Eddie gets his door keys from a side pocket of his rucksack, I fan my hands out to my side, palm down, and let my focus run down to the ground. It's like I can feel the gravel, even though I'm not touching it. And then, while I chew down on my jaw to concentrate my focus, I'm certain that the stones start to churn and rattle. I get an electric thrill just thinking about how Eddie is going to react, what he's going to say.

'Do you want a drink?' he asks, leading me through into his spacious kitchen.

'I'm OK,' I lie. My throat is parched.

'You sure?' Eddie goes to a cupboard and pulls out a glass before going to the fridge for some juice. He still seems very worried about me.

'Well, if you're having some,' I say.

Eddie pours the juice for me before going to get himself another glass.

'So, are you going to tell me what's going on or what?' he says finally, propping himself up on the kitchen countertop.

'Is anyone else home?' I ask, cautious.

'Mum won't be long with Merry, and my big bro is back from uni at the moment. He's meant to be reading for his dissertation, but I swear he just seems to spend all his time sleeping.'

'Can we go to your room then?'

'Look, mate, I know that you said in the car that everything was fine... but seriously... is it? What's going on? You're making me worry. And what the hell were you doing on the roof?'

'Let's go to your room and I'll tell you everything.'

Eddie arches a single eyebrow and nods, before leading me up the kitchen stairs. Yes, he has a separate staircase in his kitchen. I suppose that it used to be the stairs servants used, but for some reason this has always felt the most decadent thing about his whole house. More so than the en-suite bathrooms and the ancient treehouse at the bottom of the garden.

The square footage of Eddie's bedroom and adjoining bathroom is probably the same as my living room and kitchen combined. In proportion to his house it's probably not that big (and actually isn't the biggest) but for me this room symbolises impossible luxury. Clean-beige walled and neutrally carpeted, with splashes of blue in the curtains and other fixtures. A significant amount of space is taken up by a double bed. On his desk is a giant flatscreen monitor that doubles as a television, and propped up in the corner is an electric guitar his brother gave him the Christmas before last, but which he still hasn't started learning to play. The room is unbelievably clean and tidy, but then Eddie doesn't have to bother with those kinds of chores; a cleaner comes who looks after all that for him. Even though Eddie has all this stuff, I know that his most precious possessions are his books. Some first editions, some signed, and some so precious he's wrapped them in cellophane, books are everywhere. Most are on shelves, but there are also piles dotted here and there (on his bedside table, on his desk, and a few random stacks against the walls). I know he hasn't read them all, but that's not the point. He's into the collecting almost as much as he's into the words inside. It helps that his mum used to work in publishing, as she got the collection started off, but now he curates it single-handedly, taking pride in the unbroken spines of unread paperbacks, and the yellowed pages of the older editions. The rows and stacks of the really old books are a little incongruous with the style of the bedroom (and the sleek modern style of the house as a whole), but it doesn't seem to matter. It's all definitely Eddie.

'I've just got to say this first, before you say anything.' Eddie sits down on the end of his bed, hugging a navy cushion in front of him. 'You should know that I really like Kesia and I'm going to ask her out. As in, you know, boyfriend and girlfriend. I'm really hoping that whatever you have to say to me, whatever *this* is, won't get in the way of that. OK?'

'Really?' I reply. I know that he's shown a lot of interest in Kesia, but has she really shown much interest back?

'Well, yes,' Eddie replies seriously. 'And, well, I like talking to her, and she likes books and all the theatre stuff, and I suppose that it's time that I got a girlfriend. Hal had already had three girlfriends by the time he was my age. I'm thinking of asking her out this weekend, or seeing if she wants to come over for dinner next week. I just . . . I wanted it all to be clear with you. And I want to say that I'd never let a girl get between our friendship. So I think it's best that, whatever you're about to say to me now, that you know that first.'

'That all sounds great, Eddie, but what do you think

66

I'm going to say to you?' I test, a little confused about why he thinks this has anything to do with Kesia.

'Look, I know it's tough sometimes and that you don't have a lot of friends at Gatford, but I value our friendship, I really do, and I wouldn't want any *new feelings* to come in between what we have already. I know that having secrets can make you scared and depressed and maybe make you think about doing things that involve . . . roofs and jumping and . . . whatever your secret is, it's important that you know that even before you say anything, that I'm still going to be your friend.'

'New feelings?'

'Not to pre-empt what it is you're going to tell me, but I just wanted to put that out there.'

'Eddie. I don't have *feelings* for you.'

'No, right . . . of course you don't.' He can't look at me, and he's nervously playing with the cushion, tugging at a loose thread, but I can't stop staring at him, because he's being rather brilliant and hilarious.

'What *did* you think I was doing up on the roof? Did you think . . . did you think that I was going to jump off because I was in love with you?'

'You aren't?'

'No! No – that would be too weird! Not because being gay is weird or wrong or anything,' I add quickly. 'But because you're Eddie, and seriously, dude, is that what you really thought?'

67

'I don't know! I literally have absolutely no idea! Why are you being so weird then?'

'*I'm* being weird?'

'Mate, I thought you were about to come out and declare your undying love for me! You've been strange these last few days, with the headaches and stuff, and I know you trying to come out with *something* all last week. I thought that maybe it was all the emotional stress. And I thought because I've admittedly been a little girl-obsessed lately... I thought I was going to have to break your heart or something! I mean... just so you know, just to put it out there... It would have been OK if you were, you know... gay. Because we're friends and these things happen sometimes, and it's not like I haven't thought about my own *interests*... from time to time... but Kesia has really confirmed things for me. I'm definitely into girls. And whatever you're into is fine too.'

'I'm also into girls! Jeez, Eddie, you know how I feel about Indira!'

'Yes, but what if that was all just a cover? I mean face it, she's basically inaccessible, when you fainted you didn't even go with her to the nurse!'

'Of course I'm interested in her. I didn't go with her to the nurse because I didn't want to look like an idiot! One day, maybe one day soon, I want to be able to impress her. Not fall at her feet... Although, to be honest, I think declaring my undying love for you might be simpler than what I really have to say...'

'Now you're scaring me...'

'You really thought I was going to say *I love you*?'

'Come on, lay off. It was a perfectly reasonable thing to assume.' He hugs the cushion close and rubs his arms in blatant embarrassment. 'Now out with it...'

I think about this one more time, give myself one more opportunity to back out. I could still do it. I could still tell him that it's nothing and not to worry, and then make my escape. I remember what Vega said on the television last week, about how she had a friend she could trust, and that made everything better. Who knows how much more I'm going to change in the near future? Can I handle it alone? And who better to rely upon than the one person who has stuck by me so far, no matter what?

Eddie has a funny little bowl of marbles on his desk, a remnant of his long-lost childhood. I reach out and pick it up, placing it down in front of me. This won't be easy, but if I did it with the gravel in his driveway, then surely I can manage this.

'What are you doing?' Eddie asks, pushing his glasses up on his nose.

'Give me a moment...this is still pretty new for me...' I say.

I close my eyes, partly to help me focus, and partly – if I'm honest – for dramatic effect. I visualise the marbles in my head and, after a beat of concentration, I start to feel for one with my invisible mind-fingers. I try to roll it around in my mind as though it was a real, tangible entity, and sure enough, when I open my eyes again, there's one perfect marble, clear and streaked with red, hovering in the air as if suspended by an invisible string. With my jaw clenched, I can even spin it around a bit. I'm concentrating so hard, and I'm so conscious of Eddie there watching me, that I almost forget to breathe. When I finally do let go, the marble falls straight back down into the bowl.

'Woah . . .' Eddie says. I don't say anything. I bite down on my lip and try to work out how he's reacting. This is entirely new territory and I have no idea what I'm meant to say.

'Did you just . . . ?' he starts. 'I mean, was that you . . . ?'

'Yup.'

'Woah.'

'I know.'

'When did you find out about this?'

'It started last week. Remember when I passed out? With Indira?'

'So it definitely wasn't about needing glasses?'

'I don't think so. I reckon the headaches were to do with this starting. Also, my asthma seems to be gone too, which I think must be another superhero thing.'

'*Superhero*?'

'Yeah, like the Vigils. This is how it starts, right?'

'I don't know,' Eddie admits. 'I watch a lot of the Vigil stuff, but weren't some of them born with their powers?'

'I think puberty might be a factor too. Did you see that new Vigil girl, Vega, on the telly last week? I think it all started for her when she became a teenager.'

'Woah...'

'You can keep this a secret, right?' I test, suddenly panicking that I might have got the whole thing between us wrong. Eddie might have been fine with the possibility of me being gay, but can I trust him with a secret as big as this?

'So are you going to be one of them? Can you fly?'

'I'm not sure. I've tried, but so far nothing. That was why I was out on the roof. I was seeing if I could shock myself into flying. But it didn't work.' I decide not to tell him about being able to see things when my eyes are closed. Despite the weirdness of the conversation, that one just feels *too* crazy to explain.

I watch him process it all, taking it in and making sure that it makes sense.

'Eddie,' I push, 'I need to know that you can keep this a secret.'

'Oh my gosh, of course you can!' And there go the floodgates of relief. 'I mean, this is huge! Potentially much huger than you being in love with me. Can you imagine? That I ever thought that you were going to...?'

'So we're cool about this?' I test again.

'Completely! But, dude . . . one marble? Is that it?'

'Hey! It's early days! And it's harder than you'd think. It sounds strange, but things are heavy in my brain in the same way that they have weight in the real world. Except, so far everything is much heavier. So lifting one marble feels like lifting a massive crate or something. It's hard work. I hope that it's like a muscle and that I'll get stronger.'

'How strong, do you think?'

'I don't know. Cars, maybe?'

'Have you tried water droplets? How would that work? And what about light particles? Couldn't you bend light to make yourself invisible?'

'Wow . . . that kind of stuff seems a little bit out of reach right now. I mean, I have tried doing stuff with water when I'm in the shower, but it's not that impressive. Maybe one day? With practice? I need to work on my breathing too. At the moment it feels like when you're trying to pat your head and rub your tummy at the same time. It's hard work, and I have to really concentrate.'

'Can you do it again? Can you try two marbles? Three?' His face has a puppy-like determination as he dives his hands into the bowl of marbles and holds out a selection for me.

I grit my teeth in anticipation and take a deep breath, this time daring myself to keep my eyes open. I can feel my eyebrows pinch together as I focus, and with my mind

I feel out a couple of the marbles and draw them up and out of his hand, willing them with all my might to rotate.

'This. Is. The. Coolest!' Eddie sighs. 'I can't wait to tell Kesia!'

'Wait – what?' The marbles suddenly drop and scatter on Eddie's floor. 'You can't tell Kesia. You can't tell *anyone*. This is a secret, between us. You said!'

'But I'm going to ask Kesia out. I'll have to tell her if she becomes my girlfriend. I want us to be a couple, one of those couples that don't keep secrets from each other.'

'Dude, you haven't even actually asked her out yet... and even so, you won't be asking her to marry you!'

'I want this to be a serious relationship.'

'Yes, but... we're talking about superpowers here. Not some stupid secret about –' think, Joseph, think – 'stuff!'

'I can't know this and not tell Kesia.'

'Please, Eddie, this has to stay between us. I can't let anybody else know. Not until I've worked out what it all means and how far this is going to go. I swear, once this is all figured out, then we'll tell people. Like my mum! At least hold off until I've told my mum.'

Eddie studies me, looking dubious.

'It hasn't even started yet and already our relationship is based on lies.' He sighs. 'This isn't cool, mate, but I'll do it. For you. This whole superpower thing will remain our little secret. Until you tell your mum. Which will be when exactly?'

'I don't know. I really don't. Vega – on the telly? – she was amazing. What I can do is like drawing stick figures compared to her painting a masterpiece. There has to be more to what I can do, I know it. I just have to learn how to control it. These things take time. You think that Quantum just woke up one morning being Quantum? I want to be good like they are when I tell my mum, and I have no idea how long that will take.'

Eddie nods, drawing his fingers together under his chin.

'Then I shall help you!' he announces.

'You will?'

'Sure. We'll figure this out. We'll soon have you flying out of Gatford and joining the London team. They'll be begging you to team up with them. You'll see!'

'Oh, thank you, Eddie. I mean it. I knew that you'd be cool.'

'Me? I'm the coolest! Now –' he dives his hand back into the bowl – 'three marbles!'

We stay in Eddie's room for well over an hour as he pushes me, and pushes me, into trying to hold up more marbles. It makes me dizzy; it makes my head hurt. Not the sharp, crackling pain of the headaches, but a dull ache like the beat of a bass drum in my skull. The more I try, the harder it becomes, and I end up annoyed with myself for not being able to do any better. Eddie doesn't seem to realise how tiring I'm finding all of this and has all the crazy energy of a bunny on Pixy Stix. Fortunately reprieve does come, in the form of Eddie's little sister Merry, who knocks on Eddie's bedroom door with an irritating *tat-tat-tat*.

'WHAT?' Eddie shouts out.

'What are you doing?'

'GO AWAY, MERRY.'

Meredith is the youngest of the Olsens, and in Year Seven. Despite being on the tiny side, she has the athletic build of the Olsen clan and exactly the same gold-brown hair as the rest. She's like the plain 'before' shot of her older sister Kitty (who is in the year below us), who now has blonde streaks and wears as much make-up as she can get away with.

'But Mum says you have to come downstairs...' she whines just beyond the door.

'I HAVE COMPANY, MERRY.'

'Mum says Joseph can stay, but you have to come downstairs right now because we're going through Hal's stuff and she wants you there because she doesn't want to throw anything away without checking if you might need it first!'

Eddie frowns and looks at me apologetically, although in truth I'm hugely relieved by the interruption.

'It's OK, I'm pretty tired anyway,' I tell him.

'Maybe we can do more stuff after dinner?' he asks.

'Or maybe I should just go home. We've done a lot – it might not seem it, but I think we have, and I'm really worn out from everything.'

Eddie gets up to go downstairs, and I follow close behind. So close, that I practically bash right into him when he stops dead after opening his bedroom door. Little Merry is standing right there on the threshold, with an expectant gleam in her eyes and a mischievous smile.

'Watcha doing in there?' she asks, all sweet and innocent.

'Nothing. We weren't doing anything. It's none of your business,' Eddie replies.

'I heard sounds.'

'What? There weren't any sounds,' Eddie insists, although thinking about it, there was some distinct clattering when I was trying to levitate some books.

'My room is right next to yours. I definitely heard things.'

For an eleven-year-old, Merry does seem particularly precocious. I stay quiet and look at my feet while Eddie tries to get her off our case.

'Out of the way, Merry. I thought you said Mum wanted me downstairs.'

She reluctantly steps aside but takes the opportunity to peer back into Eddie's room to see if she can spy the cause of the commotion. Mostly Eddie's siblings are great, but there are moments like this when I'm thankful that I'm an only child.

When we get downstairs Eddie heads straight for the front room, where Hal, the eldest of all the Olsens, appears to be napping on one of the long sofas. In the middle of the room are piles and piles of stuff (packed boxes and crates and other assorted full containers). It might have all been here when Eddie and I got in, but we went straight into the kitchen and didn't notice. Almost completely hidden among all the stuff is Eddie's mum, who looks busy and flustered.

'Eddie!' she calls, perking her head up when we come into the room.

I like Mrs Olsen, because she's always busy doing something. She calls herself a lady of leisure, but that makes me think of someone who wears pearls and lies around on a chaise longue eating grapes. That's not what Jemima Olsen is like. She's feisty and intelligent and always *doing things*. She raises money for charities and sits on parent committees at school, plus she rides horses and plans galas and generally just about manages to organise all of her children. I've never once actually seen her 'at leisure', and right now is just another one of those occasions. She's ruddy-faced and dwarfed by boxes, while her first-born just lies there on the sofa, apparently worn out and oblivious.

'Mum, what are you doing?' Eddie asks.

'We're going through Hal's stuff!' Jem announces. 'We'll probably give a lot of it to charity, but before we do I thought I'd see if there's anything you need. Ski boots? Riding jacket? Golf clubs?'

I know for a fact that Eddie neither skis, rides nor has ever been anywhere near a golf course.

'Joseph!' Jem cries, seeing me lingering shyly in the doorway. 'Is there anything you need?'

It's incredibly nice of Jem to offer, but I would never, ever take anything from the Olsens. She knows that. What use could I possibly have for Hunter wellies, or fishing rods, or cummerbunds?

'Is Hal OK?' Eddie asks, heading over to his apparently

78

comatose brother and poking him with an outstretched foot. 'Has uni really killed him this time?'

'Go away,' Hal groans, not even bothering to open his eyes.

I head further into the living room, but am careful not to touch anything. I peer over some of the containers, pretending to look interested, just to be polite.

'Please, Joseph, if there's anything you need ... We're literally just going to give it all away anyway.' I know Jem doesn't mean to make me sound like a charity case, but I feel it regardless.

Then I see something.

At first I think that it must be for Halloween. It's a white mask, with the entire frontpiece made from stiff, white gauze. I reach to pick it up, forgetting that I'm meant to just be acting polite.

'Oh, do you fence, Joseph?' Jem asks.

'Fence?' I ask back.

'That's a fencing mask,' Eddie explains. 'Hal was really into fencing for all of five minutes. Which means we've got all the kit you could possibly ever need or want.'

'Try it on!' Merry yips, coming into the room and landing on the sofa, squashing Hal's legs as she does so. He emits a wound-up groan and covers his face with his arm.

'Can I?' I check with Jem.

'Of course!' she replies.

I slip the mask over my head. I would have thought that

the inside would be a musty stew of Hal's hair products and grease, but it's practically new. The mask must have rarely, if ever, been worn. It's a bit tough at first, but after a tug I manage to pull it down over my face until it's snug.

'Want to try on the chest guard too?' Jem offers.

'I'm OK, thanks,' I reply, my voice muffled through the gauze. I turn to Eddie: 'Can you tell that it's me?'

'Nope. Your head just looks like an egg,' he replies.

Yet I can see him perfectly. You wouldn't think it, because from the outside the gauze looks completely opaque, but from my side the view is barely restricted at all. It must be like the stuff that costume characters wear at theme parks that allows them to see out but nobody else to see in, except even tougher because the mask is designed to protect the face from pointy swords. Bonus points for it not being even remotely stinky!

'You're not going to join the fencing club, are you?' Eddie moans.

'No,' I reply.

'Then why do you want it?' he asks.

I try and signal to him that there's a perfectly good reason for me needing and wanting this mask, but of course he can't see my facial expressions at all. And, Eddie being Eddie, he hasn't put two and two together yet either.

'Oh, it's just a bit of fun, you know?' I reply, when I realise that Jem and Merry are looking at me weirdly.

'You never know when something like this might come in handy!'

'Then you simply must take it,' Jem determines. 'And you must have the rest of the kit too. It wouldn't be proper to split it all up anyway.'

'I couldn't,' I say, tugging at the mask to try to take it off. In the end it requires Eddie to come to my rescue, and even then it takes a couple of good heaves.

'Joseph, have the mask. If you want to take up fencing, then you mustn't let my lazy son put you off,' Jem says.

'Oh, well . . . if you're really sure?' I don't want to appear too needy, even though I already know that the mask is mine.

'Of course!' Jem coos. 'Let me go get a bag for you to take it all in!'

'Seriously, mate, why do you want that mask?' Eddie ponders.

'Because . . .' I say, looking sternly at him, 'reasons.'

Eddie looks back at me, cocking his head over to one side. He really doesn't get it.

'If you get a sword, can I play with it?' Merry giggles. I ignore her.

'You know why I want it.' I focus on Eddie, willing him to catch my drift. 'For that thing . . .'

'What thing?'

'You know, the thing . . . with the marbles?'

'The marbles?' There's a pause, and I let it sit, waiting

81

for the realisation to click. 'Oh! The marbles!' There it is. 'Yes! I see what you mean. The mask would be perfect for that!'

'You guys are weird,' Merry muses.

Looking down at it again, I can almost imagine a face in the gauze. When people see me in this mask, and maybe the whole outfit (I'll have to try it on later and see what I think), they won't see Wilco the walkover, they'll see someone they need to actually pay some attention to. Behind this mask, I might be able to become the person I want to be. It's all coming together. I might even end up a real hero.

'And now! The continuing adventures of Fencing-Mask Boy!' I say at myself in the mirror. 'No, that's not right.'

Hands on hips, I stare down at my feet, as if somehow my scuffed school shoes will give me the inspiration I need. Looking back up at myself, I'm learning not to be startled by the sight of the mask and the 'egg-ness' of my head. I've got my black hoodie on again, and with the hood pulled up I look like a character from a creepy Japanese film.

'Beware, the fantastical might of Eggface!'

That doesn't work either.

'Egghead?' I try.

No, definitely not.

The school toilets might not be the best place to try to

figure out my superhero codename, but Eddie has promised that he'll come and help me practise my powers as soon as maths club is over. I was going to go to the library and get on with some homework, but to be honest, the thought of wearing the mask again has made me twitchy with anticipation. Knowing that it's there in my bag, waiting to be used, has haunted me all through the school day, and I couldn't wait any longer to have the chance of trying it on again.

I put on the rest of the fencing outfit when I got home from Eddie's house last night, and let's just say I don't think it would have worked as an ensemble. The top had this weird strap that went in between the legs and wasn't exactly the most comfortable thing in the world, besides which, Hal is a little taller than me and everything was coming up big and baggy. The mask on its own though? Very cool, and does the job of hiding my true identity perfectly. Plus I feel taller somehow, my shoulders broader, even though nothing else has changed. It's as if, by hiding who I really am, I can become whoever I want to be. Someone braver, and someone better. I wonder if this is what the Vigils feel like, in their costumes and masks.

A conversation is happening outside. The voices continue a tiny bit longer by the door to the toilets, giving me the chance to dash into a cubicle and hide. I put the lid down and crouch down on top of the toilet so that nobody will catch me. I might not be breaking any rules, but something tells me that being discovered after school looking like this and talking to myself in the mirror would hardly go down well.

'La la la, dee da dee...' It's Dr Lane.

Technically he shouldn't even be using these toilets; the ones for the teachers (which I imagine are much better cared for) are just down the hallway, but I guess this one is closer to his classroom, and it's not as if he expects anyone to be around at this time. Head of music, Dr Lane is a Gatford institution – I've heard people say that he's been here ever since the school was founded over a century ago, and it wouldn't surprise me if that was true. Old-fashioned in every way, Dr Lane is precisely the type of person I don't want finding me in here. He's always taken a perverse pleasure in dishing out detentions with little provocation. So he's not going to think twice about giving me one if he finds me in here after hours, especially with a mask.

He uses one of the urinals, then goes to wash his hands, singing his little ditty the entire time.

'La dee, la daa...'

This new vision thing is really weird. I'm hiding in the stall, keeping myself as quiet as possible, and there's no way I should be able to see him, and yet Dr Lane is clear as crystal in my head. It's not just my imagination. I have to really focus, but it's like my mind can zoom up and over the stall door, so that I can see the lines on his face, the disgusting little dabs of dried saliva-yuck in the corners of his mouth and, most extraordinarily, the toupee on his head.

I wasn't even sure that it was a toupee when I first started at Gatford. I mean, people said that it was, but I guess that I've always been a little naive about these kinds of things. Why anyone would bother covering up their bald head with a wig is beyond me. You're going bald, so what? All things considered, Dr Lane's one isn't actually that bad, but it's the kind of thing that once you suss out, you can't ever forget about. You can see it in the way that the grey at his temples is a little different from the grey on top, and how there's an undercut line at the back of his head where the toupee doesn't quite blend in to the hair that is still there. When he has his back to the class, and is writing on the board, you can gaze at it for ever, just imagining what his hair must be like underneath. Well, I guess now is finally the time for me to find out.

Feeling through the fibres of the toupee, I can instantly tell that it's not real hair. It's far silkier and smoother than the hair that's at the nape of his neck, which is course and brittle. I squeeze my eyes shut and clench my fists and slowly, carefully, I work at tugging the toupee away from his head.

'What the blazes?' Dr Lane exclaims, watching in the mirror as his rug rises into the air.

He just stands there, amazed for a short moment, as

his hairpiece shudders and hovers until it resembles a sort of hairy halo. Then, all of a sudden, he brings up both hands and pulls the toupee back down, keeping one hand there as he races out of the toilet, whimpering something about poltergeists.

Coming out of the stall, I rest against one of the sinks, glancing up to check my masked reflection in the mirror. I'm exhausted. The amount of focus and concentration I had to use has practically winded me, so I guess that I still can't use these powers for very long. Which sucks.

I might have only had the toupee off his head for a short time, but what I glimpsed under there was hilarious. A comb-over. One of those really lame ones where he's let the hair on one side grow ridiculously long so that it covers the baldness and reaches right over to the other side. Why he needs such a drastic comb-over when nobody is ever going to see it is baffling, but there we are. I can't wait to tell Eddie!

'And I swear it just flew off my head!' Dr Lane is coming back in, along with someone else.

Damn it. Not enough time to hide again. They're already in here by the time I've even clocked them.

'Hey!' Dr Lane exclaims, seeing me stunned in front of him. 'Who the devil do you think you are?'

Without even thinking, I run for it. Dr Lane tries to catch me, but I'm too fast for him (this isn't because I'm particularly fast, but more because Dr Lane is incredibly slow) and his companion, Mr Schuster, is too shocked to do anything. I whip past them both and zoom out of the door. They haven't had a chance to see me properly because of the mask, but I don't want to hang around where I can be caught again.

I dash down the corridor and around the corner, almost certain that I'm not being chased but unwilling to stop anyway, just in case. I round another corner, not bothering to think ahead and definitely not checking where I am going, so that when I burst through a set of double doors I manage to smack right into someone who is carrying a large amount of hockey sticks.

It's only as they all fall to the floor that I realise who it is: Indira.

7

'Get off me, you freak!' Indira cries as I scramble back up to my feet.

I accidentally grab her bare leg (she's in her hockey skirt) as I try to find my balance, and I'm so embarrassed that I reach out to touch her again, just to say sorry. But I can't speak, there aren't any words there. So instead I stumble backwards again, my wrists taking the brunt of the fall this time, and if I wasn't wearing the mask she would clearly be able to see that my face has turned scorching red.

'What is wrong with you?' she's saying as she pulls herself backwards away from me, fumbling for one of the many hockey sticks now littered around us.

There's a flash of realisation that she might want to hit me with one of the sticks, so like a cat with lightning reflexes, I instinctively bring a palm up and push all of them away with my mind so that they scatter away across the corridor. It's so instinctual and so quick that for a moment I can't quite believe that I've managed to exert that much power. Once I've recovered from the shock of being able to move so many things so far away, I look back at Indira and realise I've made a wrong move. A very wrong move.

'What the hell?' she says, pushing a dark strand of hair out of her eyes and looking around in shock.

Why didn't I just stand up and apologise for bashing into her like a normal person? Instead I had to go and make an exhibition of myself, use my meagre powers to draw attention to myself. Besides which my head is now throbbing from the exertion.

'Did you just...?' Indira ponders, a slight shake in her voice. To which I respond with a shrug. The ridiculous, embarrassing shrug of a socially inept idiot.

But still, she looks impressed. So I bring my palm back up and, almost in a daze because the headache is humming through my temples, I attempt to pick one of the hockey sticks back up. It's the biggest thing I've attempted to levitate so far, and I'm terrified that I won't be able to hold it, but I push through because I'm desperate to impress Indira some more. I'm dying for her to be impressed actually, and this far outweighs my desire to escape.

The stick hovers and wobbles around in a rickety fashion as Indira watches, and soon I have it in front of her, ready for her to pluck it out of the air. She doesn't take it straight away. She's still on the floor for starters, plus she's quite obviously weirded out. She stays completely still and watches, her gaze flickering from the floating stick, then to my mask, and then back to the stick again. The only problem with all this quiet watching is that now I'm really struggling to hold on, but I'm also too petrified to speak to her, so the stick just hangs there as awkwardly as our silence.

'Are you doing this?' she asks me, her voice quiet like a secret.

I nod, my jaw clenched as I struggle to keep the sticks hovering, but she can't tell. The mask hides all of my pain and anguish.

'How?' she asks.

This I can't answer, even if I wanted to. I incline my head down, teeth grinding with the effort, and will her to take the stick. Finally, achingly, she does, and I can let go.

'Who are you?' Her voice is soft, awestruck, as she stands up to meet me at eye level.

We're about the same height, with me only just taller, so once she's standing and facing me I can look directly at her. Her face is so symmetrical, so perfect.

There's a beat of silence, with something definitely fizzing in the air between us, but I'm terrified of doing anything that might ruin the moment. I shrug a sigh (of hope? Of longing? I don't know) and then I turn and run. Without looking I know that she's still standing there, among the rest of the discarded hockey sticks, completely stunned and immobile.

I was meant to wait for Eddie, but I text him my excuses and take the bus home. All the way I'm thinking about Indira. As I make dinner and do my homework: Indira. I somehow manage to read a whole chapter of *Jane Eyre* without taking any of it in, because: Indira. I just can't believe that it's possible to feel this way about another person and not have them feel the same way back. Except...she doesn't know it's me. She can't know it's me, not yet. Not until I'm better, and stronger, and able to stand up to kids like Godfrey. There was definitely a moment between us. I wasn't imagining it. Different from when she helped me in the memorial garden. Very different. Because I'm different, and I can't help but imagine that as my powers grow, so will that force between us. I'm determined to be worthy of her. I want to be as smart as Deep Blue, as fearless as Quantum, and have Solar's impish wit. Just a few days ago these seemed like impossible dreams. But now? Now anything is possible. I don't have to be Wilco for ever, I can be something else, something better. And reap all the rewards that come with that.

The next day goes by in a bit of a haze. I look up at every person who comes into any room, wondering if it might be her. I look for her in hallways, search for her in the dining hall (eyes down so that it's not obvious, using my weird psychic vision thing to hover around every table), and pace the memorial garden, looking out over the cage where the others play football, just in case she might happen to walk by. Despite this, I only manage to catch a proper sight of her once, at lunch, when she's in the middle of a huddle with her girlfriends. What's she talking about? Is she telling them? Do they all know about me?

The final lesson of the next day is double PE. It comes around once every two weeks, and is always my worst nightmare. Especially now that the days are getting warmer and sunnier. So far all our PE lessons this term have been indoors, which means sometimes, if I'm lucky, I can get away with messing around at the ping-pong table while the other boys compete on the rowing machines or try out a bit of basketball. But now that it's definitely spring, the regular double session means torture.

The official Gatford House PE kit is not designed for boys like me. It involves a dark green and navy polo shirt and navy shorts, which might not sound all that bad, except that these shorts seem designed to flatter the really muscley boys with super-strong thighs from all the years of vigorous sports they've been playing. On a kid like me, my legs just look like pale twigs, and there's far too much thigh exposed for anyone's liking. Yup, these shorts are short-shorts. Plus, mine appear to be at least three shades lighter than everyone else's, owing to the fact that mine are second- (or maybe even third-) hand. Same goes for the shirt too: washed out compared to the vivid intensity of everyone else's. I hate the fact that all the kids watching us from their classroom windows can tell my status, despite being miles away, all because my kit has been through the wash more times.

Despite the dry spell, it's still breezy and cold, but we're not allowed to wear our Gatford hoodies as apparently that wouldn't make us resilient. So instead my goose-pimpled skin turns almost as blue as my faded shorts. The only good thing about this whole wretched endeavour is that, for the first time in my life, I can actually breathe unaided through a whole lesson. Something about me is definitely changing.

'Doing well there, Wilco!' Mr Armstrong calls after me as we run a couple of warm-up laps around the pitch. And yes, even the teachers call me Wilco. There's no point in trying to correct them. The teachers here, especially the sporty ones, hate to call anybody by their actual given names. It's like a secret posh-school rule that they don't tell you about beforehand.

One lap around, and for once I'm not at the back. I'm not nearly as tired as I should be.

'What have they put in your water, Wilco?' Mr Armstrong calls as I pass him on my second lap. I know that what I'm doing isn't exactly impressive (I'm still in the middle of the pack) but I can't say that I'm not a little pleased that he's noticing my progress, and I run a bit faster.

'Just some new treatment for the asthma, sir!' I call back, overtaking someone else.

Shouldn't I be tired now? I'm pretty certain that I should be – but my legs are pumping, my breathing is loose and my throat is clear. I've overtaken quite a few people and I'm a little gutted that nobody else in my class has noticed my obvious progress, but still, this is pretty amazing. Usually I'd be red-faced, sweaty and just about ready to keel over by this point. I'd be reaching for my inhaler and puffing away like my life depended on it. I suppose it's weird that practising my powers manages to knock me out, and yet I'm stronger at jogging than I've ever been. My body is weirding me out, but there's definitely something exciting going on.

I find myself standing up straight and revelling in my new-found wellness, smiling around at the other boys as if I could actually be considered a peer and not an underling. But the smile is washed off my face pretty quickly, as soon as Mr Armstrong says the two magic words: 'cross country'.

Whatever was in me that was feeling light and buoyant plummets so that a wave of nausea rises up and crashes through my stomach. Cross country is the worst, and no matter how well my body appears to be doing right now, that doesn't stop the intrinsic sense of dread and horror.

It's at least a solid hour of jogging, and if you're caught even thinking about slowing down and walking, you can end up in detention. Far beyond the school grounds there are fields and ditches and scrubland that will have already been marked out with cones so that we can find our way. I know why Mr Armstrong has chosen today: the ground is dry and solid, and because it's the last lesson of the day, it means we're all expected to complete the course, however long it takes. Even if it takes for ever, Mr Armstrong will be there at the finish line, ready and waiting to humiliate as necessary.

'Attention, this way, boys!' Mr Armstrong calls. 'The ten of you with the worst time will be doing the whole thing again next time. And don't think I won't hold you to it!' We don't. We all know he will.

Another stomach lurch, another pang of fear, and another quick look at the boys around me. They're jogging on the spot, puffing their chests out and stretching their arms. Godfrey's eyes are gleaming with the thrill of the chase. He's not the fastest runner in the pack, but he knows that he's going to be making a good time. As do his friends. They look like they're psyching themselves up to jump off the top diving board, full of drive and adrenaline and looking forward to the pain.

Eddie stands next to me and gives me a reassuring smile. I know that he's thinking of waiting for me and running at my pace, but I shake my head at him,

95

acknowledging the offer but indicating that he should run for himself. I know he can cope with a race like this no problem. He once told me that it's like acting: all he has to do is pretend that he is an athlete, and the inspiration will come. Eddie's like that. He's good at anything he turns his mind to. I can see him doing it now, preparing himself and getting into character.

Just behind me is Fat Henry, the only other one in the class who I know will be dreading the race as much as me. His face is already red and sweaty from the warm-up, and his eyes skitter about nervously, searching for any way that he might be able to get out of it. If we had been given some warning of this lesson, I'm pretty sure Henry would have a sick note ready and waiting. To be honest, I'd probably have a sick note lined up too. But here we are, stuck on this field under a high white sky, with no visible way out.

Mr Armstrong sets us up on the start line and tells us to do one more final stretch before letting us go. Godfrey and his minions are laughing. What could they possibly have to laugh about before one of the hardest trials it's possible to do in a PE class?

I'm still looking around me, almost frantic as I try to think of any way I can get out of this (fake a sprained ankle? Take a tumble right near the start? Pray for one of my blackout headaches?) when the whistle goes. All the other boys, even Henry, shoot off across the field. They're meant to be pacing themselves so that they can cope with the whole route.

'Go on, Wilco! Put some welly into it!' I can hear Mr Armstrong call behind me – and I do.

Like in the warm-up earlier, I soon find that I can hit a stride that is bearable, and before I know it I'm overtaking people again. A lot of people. At this rate I needn't worry about being in the bottom ten. At this rate I'll soon be catching Eddie and maybe even Godfrey up!

The land rises ahead of me, before sloping down again into a shallow valley. I can't see what's ahead as the hill dips away, but I can make out one of the bright orange cones that marks the path. *This will be OK*, I tell myself. *I can do this*. Indira's face blazes in my head, and I think about how much more impressed with me she'd be if I was as physically fit as the other boys. *Maybe this should be a new life goal. Maybe if I went for a jog every day after school this might actually work for me*...And then I see them.

It's Godfrey and three of his mates, standing just away from the path, within a little copse of freshly budding trees. And they're smoking. They're passing a cigarette between them, taking long drags before passing it on. As I get closer, I realise that something in the air isn't quite right; the smell isn't the usual tobacco scent that I'm familiar with.

What I should do is continue at my steady pace and not even turn my head in their direction. I should pretend that they're invisible, and if anyone asks me afterwards, I never even saw them. But my horror at seeing them, and my confusion at the sweet smell, means that I stumble. Not so much that I fall over, but enough to make Godfrey look my way, and realise that I've spotted him.

'Hey, Wilco!' he calls after a pause. 'What are you on? Shouldn't you be at the back crying or something?'

I ignore him and continue jogging; I even turn up the pace. I want to get away. I want to pretend that I haven't seen anything and, more than anything, I just want this stupid race to be over.

'Wilco!' one of the other lads, William Prudent, calls after me. 'Where you going? We've got some unfinished business with you.'

So the Titler business hasn't been forgotten. Damn! I sense the chase beginning. Whatever instinct it is that tells a creature it has become prey, and that the predator is close behind, kicks in and propels me onwards. My legs burn, and my lungs ache, but I know that, above all, I have to escape before the bigger boys get me. I will my new-found speed and fitness to get me away from them.

But I know my plan is doomed to fail. Because these boys are faster, and better, and are nearly on top of me before I've even had a chance to finish the thought.

One second I am running, and the next I'm flying. My arm is yanked and I'm flung off the path, the speed at which I'm going used against me as I tumble over and into a nearby ditch. Despite there having been no rain lately, the ground still feels damp, and my hands and arse seem to have found the only patch of mud in the vicinity. I don't even stop when I land. Instead I slide, and when I try to buoy myself up, I just slip back instead. I'm panting, all my limbs feel out of place, and standing right over me, his head silhouetted against the afternoon sun, is Godfrey.

They're clever enough not to hit me anywhere it might show. Apparently shins are fair game though. I know this because mine feel radioactive with pain. I suppose the thinking is that they can say I fell over and my lower legs took the brunt. My fingers grip down into the mud as Godfrey kicks me in the side. He's a good kicker. Lots of practice on the field. One of the other lads – another William (there are about five in my year) – stands a bit away, staring daggers at the stragglers coming up behind me so that no one interferes. I suppose I should feel lucky that nobody's got their phones with them, because I can just imagine how this might go down on YouTube.

I bite down on my lip to stop myself from screaming out, and taste blood. The ghost of my asthma, like a phantom limb in my lungs, means I automatically start coughing. I feel like I'm retching up my own insides with every groan and splutter of phlegm.

'I didn't see anything, I swear!' I manage to pant out.

'And I'm sorry about your essay. It was a mistake!' But Godfrey clearly doesn't care.

'Damn right you didn't see anything, you little runt!' he puffs back at me.

'Mate, we should get going,' William Prudent says.

'This one has been winding me up for ages,' grunts Godfrey. 'Gatford might let the weeds in, but it's our job to keep up with the pruning. Am I right?'

I wince and start to cry. Not my best moment, and the boys delight in it. I'm aware of all the other boys running past and pretending they haven't seen anything. Even Fat Henry's gone by.

'Bet he pisses himself too,' the other William laughs.

'And this –' Godfrey stands back and wallops one final kick in my side – 'is for Titler. Don't ever pull a stunt like that again. Remember who you're dealing with and have a little respect next time, Wilco.'

All I manage in reply is a weak moan. I want to gather myself up and hold myself in a ball until all the pain goes away. But then I also know that the longer I stay here, the more trouble it's going to cause in the long run. Stay here, and Mr Armstrong comes out looking for me, discovers I've been beaten up and left for dead, and Godfrey gets in trouble (I don't know if there's any other way that I could possibly explain it). And if I get Godfrey in trouble, I'm pretty sure that the next time he gets me alone he will actually kill me. Which leaves option two: get myself up, go back to Gatford and tell Mr Armstrong that I tripped and fell. There's no way I can finish the course now.

I stagger to my feet as the boys sprint away, racing ahead now so that they don't end up in the bottom ten. I'm clutching my side, and I feel like a newborn horse on wobbly stick legs, but I'm up. My head swims with stars and I can barely reach full height because my inclination is to huddle myself over and comfort my maybe-broken ribs.

Every step makes me wince, but I slowly head back the way I came, hoping that my injuries mean Mr Armstrong will go easy on me. My timing is perfect. As I scramble over the stile and back on to Gatford land, I can see the frontrunners in the race on the other side of the field, sprinting towards the finish line. Mr Armstrong applauds all of them, then starts shaking his head when he sees me, as if he can't even be bothered.

'What the hell happened to you, Wilco?' he asks as I approach. 'Given up again?'

'Fell,' I splutter, folding in over myself as I come to a stop.

The boys around me look like they've barely had to exert themselves at all to complete the course. They smack each other on the back and grab one of the bottles of water Mr Armstrong has brought out for them.

'Go get yourself cleaned up and changed,' Mr Armstrong sighs at me. Everything about his tone suggests that he's not even angry at me, just immensely disappointed.

I head back to the changing rooms, past the girls who've been playing netball, wincing in embarrassment as well as pain. I thank all the gods in the universe that Indira isn't among them. I must look a right state and I don't want any more of her pity.

If there's one thing I hate more than PE it's the PE changing rooms. Somehow I've managed to avoid using the changing-room showers for my whole time at Gatford. Some of the guys love to shower. I suspect they get as muddy as possible especially but I have always stayed as far as I could from anything that would require me to have to wash afterwards.

In fact, avoiding needing to have a shower at school has become a particular gift of mine. But getting dressed back into my school uniform is a constantly depressing struggle, knowing that somebody might be looking, and judging, and knowing that what I have is less than perfect. I mean, look at these guys: they're only just hitting their mid-teens, and yet they already have thick necks, vast expanses of shoulders and taut stomach muscles. My body consists of a pale flatness, and if you're especially lucky, you might get to see my ribs protrude. Even Eddie, who is just as skinny as me, has year-round tanned skin from all his holidays and a certain leanness that only comes from a lifetime of optimum nutrition and playing outdoors.

He comes into the changing room after me and doesn't hesitate in taking his top off.

'What happened to you?' he asks, seeing me sitting on the bench under the hooks, poking at the parts of my shins and knees that will almost certainly come up in bruises.

'Nothing,' I say pointedly, hoping that he'll be able to infer my meaning.

'Right... Well, you look terrible. And how did you get back here before me? You didn't give up, did you?'

'Didn't complete the circuit,' I admit. 'I ran into some trouble before I even got halfway.'

Before I can say any more, Godfrey and the two Williams come in. They stop when they see me, a broken mess, and then use their elbows to nudge each other before laughing. They actually laugh. I think that's the worst thing. More than their callous violence, it's the fact that they don't seem to have any realisation that they might have hurt me. Godfrey is the worst. His eyes practically gleam with self-satisfaction as I just sit there, silent and scared. They head into the shower. I should probably have one too, considering the state I'm in, but I can't be in there with them, especially while they're laughing and flicking each other with their towels. I figure that I should be able to cope through the bus journey home and I'll just have a long soak in the bath when I get there.

I don't stand up while I get changed back into my uniform. By sitting down the entire time, I draw less attention to myself. I don't even stop to check my wounds – there'll be time for that later. I can hear Godfrey laughing in the shower, the loud, rollicking laugh of someone who just doesn't care, and I feel the anger rising up within me.

'It shouldn't be allowed,' I grumble as I fix my tie.

'What?' Eddie asks.

'Godfrey. And his friends. They shouldn't be allowed to just get away with whatever they want.'

'What did they do?'

I go up to the nearby mirror to check my face. My lip has stopped bleeding from where I bit into it, but it still feels sore and bruised. Eddie comes up next to me to check his collar and tie.

'Eddie, what if there was something I could actually do with this power thing?' I say to him softly, making sure that nobody around can hear us.

'Like what? Fling a marble in his face?'

'No, nothing stupid like that. Something real. Something that teaches him a lesson.'

'Dude, seriously. All we have are marbles.'

'I'll get stronger though. I could try bigger things.' I think of Indira and the hockey stick. 'I just have to do something. I can't sit here and take it from them for one minute longer.'

105

'This trouble out on cross country – it wasn't a fall, was it?'

I look at Eddie's reflection in the mirror and give a barely noticeable shake of my head.

'Sorry, mate, that's rough.'

'It's not just me though. It's the power they have across the whole school. Those rugby boys think they're kings and can get away with anything! And if we don't like it, they'll just hit out to make sure we shut up. Look, I know Gatford is tough and there are always going to be bullies, but don't you think sometimes that we could make this place better? That if only someone would stand up to it all, it would make this school a better place?'

'Yes, but . . . you're not a Vigil,' Eddie warns me, keeping his voice low.

'I know, I know . . .' But even as I run my fingers through my mangled hair, I'm adding a silent 'not yet'. 'It's just that sometimes—'

'We cool, Wilco?' Godfrey comes up right behind me, clamps his hands down on my shoulders and smiles at me in the mirror.

I don't say anything. I set my jaw and dare myself to look back at him, to not shy away.

'That's what I thought.' He laughs. 'You're a good sport, you know that, Wilco? A damn good sport. Let's hope you stay that way, all right?'

When his buddies come over and start laughing about some private joke, Godfrey lets me go to join them.

'Was that a threat?' I ask Eddie after they've gone.

'No...well, I mean...Probably not?' Eddie tries.

'I mean it. I could do something about him. He can't be allowed to get away with hurting people. Nobody should.' And I do mean it. I'm sick of bullies and of feeling helpless. I think about my dad, how he made my mum feel so small. Why should we just accept things like that? Why can't we fight back?

'He's Godfrey Chappell,' Eddie says. 'He's always been like that. And what with his dad being a politician...What do you even think you could do?'

'Nothing big, nothing to hurt – obviously. But there must be something...just to make him scared. To make him sorry.'

'I don't know, Joseph...'

'Let me think about it. I can practise, and get better,' I insist, heading back over to the bench to get my stuff. 'Before he attacked me I was actually running pretty well. The best I've ever run. Something's happening to me. I'm changing. I'm getting stronger.'

Eddie checks his phone. 'Is that the time?'

'I thought chess club was yesterday. What are you doing after school today?'

'I have a date with Kesia!'

'A date? A proper date?'

'Well, not a date like to the cinema or anything. We're just meeting after school so that I can help her catch up with English. But I'm going to ask her out. I'm definitely going to ask her. It's just a matter of picking the right moment.' He sighs. 'But ring me later, if you have any ideas about You Know Who. Or want to practise with the marbles. Or whatever.'

He grabs his stuff and dashes out, right past Mr Armstrong, who has come in to the changing room to check that we're all ready to go as he wants to lock up.

'Come on, don't you have homes to get to?' he moans. 'And you –' he points right at me – 'don't think you're getting out of cross country, Mr Wilkes. Next double lesson we have, you'll be running the whole way around. And if I'm in a bad mood, you'll be running it twice!'

'Yes, sir,' I manage to mumble as I make my escape.

I don't bother putting my Gatford blazer back on. I have my black zip-up hoodie in my bag, brought in case PE turned out to be a particularly cold one (you're meant to have the official Gatford hoodie in official Gatford colours, but, because it's me and everyone knows I'm the scholarship kid, nobody minds if I just wear a plain one) and once I'm outside I zip it up over my collar.

Indira is chatting with her friends by the school gates. I watch her for a few seconds, feeling my heart skipping all over the place, hanging back because I don't want her to see me looking so rough. I'm pretty sure that nothing

Godfrey did to me shows, but it's more than that. It's the cloud of residual anger that I have in my head, the humiliation behind my eyes and the tension in my fists. If she's ever going to fall in love with me, it'll be when I'm confident and courageous and happy. Not when I'm a beaten-up mess. I know that Eddie says that girls have this maternal instinct and like to care, but I don't want it to be like that between us. I don't want Indira to ever think that she needs to protect me.

It's when I see Godfrey emerge from a side building, with only one William by his side, that I think maybe she's the one who needs protecting. Indira says goodbye to her girlfriends, all hugs and air kisses, as Godfrey draws near, shoulders back and smile sly.

'Bye, mate,' I hear Godfrey say to William Prudent, who walks off with Indira's friends, leaving just the two of them. Neither looks particularly happy.

'Have you got it then?' Indira says to him. I'm lucky I could catch it. Whenever a car speeds along the road I can't hear anything between them.

I'm standing by the main entrance to the school, hiding behind the columned portico, but when I close my eyes and really concentrate, I find that my vision can curl around the column and zoom right in on the two of them. I'm watching their conversation as if I was standing right there. I don't trust Godfrey with her. He's obviously still high after the fun he's had with me, and whenever he looks directly at Indira I get the sense that he's hungry. A horrible, carnal type of hunger that just makes me more and more determined to keep an eye out and make sure that he doesn't do anything to her. Would he? I mean, beating me up is one thing, but he wouldn't hurt Indira, surely? I feel a pang of worry as I see her friends get further and further away and the rest of the crowds peter out as students head off home. If only some of them had stayed with her. If only she wasn't alone with him.

'Come on, hand it over,' Indira reiterates to Godfrey.

'You really think that I'm just going to give it back to you, just like that?'

'Come on, Godders, this is me, not one of your stupid mates. I don't want any drama. Just hand it back and this can all be over.'

'As simple as that?'

'Is there a reason that it has to be complicated?'

Their conversation fades out as a truck passes, and then I have to pull myself away as a couple of teachers leave the main building, laden with stacks of papers and books, and want to know why I'm hanging around.

'Just waiting for a friend,' I say, and they leave. They obviously don't care what I'm doing, more focused on getting themselves away from the school.

I go back to Indira and Godfrey. They're closer now. He has his arms draped over her shoulders and clasped

110

behind her head. It looks pretty comfortable for him, but like a lock on her.

'Come on,' he's saying. I wish I knew what they were talking about.

'Not here, not now,' says Indira, looking irritated and uncomfortable. And something about the way she's standing reminds me of my mum in those dark days.

He pulls her head towards him and they kiss. But it's not a real kiss. It's not romantic or easy. It looks flat, and fake, and too reliant on him holding her face close.

'Stop,' Indira manages to say, attempting to pull herself away from him.

My estimation of Godfrey has descended to levels that I didn't even think were possible. It's one thing to pick on me, but something else entirely to pick on her. Not on Indira.

I'm doing it before I even think about it. My rucksack is off my back and my hand is inside, reaching for the fencing mask. I have no plan, and no concept of consequences; I just know that Indira could do with a hero right now, and that hero might be me.

9

Having any sort of practical plan would be the sensible thing, but who ever said I was sensible? My rucksack is dumped by the side of the school entrance, my hoodie is zipped up tight so that no hint of my uniform is visible and I'm charging down the driveway towards where Godfrey still has Indira entangled in his arms.

'Let her go,' I say, keeping my voice low so that they don't instantly recognise it.

He drops his arms, more out of surprise than anything else. I take in Indira's expression; she's stunned too, but she recognises me from yesterday. She doesn't say anything, but I can tell that she's not scared any more.

I try to ignore the aching throughout my body. When I move, even when I breathe, the slightest shift seems to send ripples of pain right the way through me. But my mind is clear. My mind feels clearer than it has done in ages, mostly because I've only got one thing to think about right now: saving Indira.

'Who the hell are you?' Godfrey splutters.

'Get away from her,' I say. He might have dropped his arms, but he's still too close for my liking.

'Seriously, who the hell do you think you are?'

'You should listen to him,' Indira murmurs, taking me in, watching me as she backs slowly away from the scene. 'You don't know what he can do.'

'Er...' Godfrey laughs. 'This is a joke, right?'

I move forward, closer to him. Indira backs further away. I get a thrill from knowing that she remembers me, that she remembers what I can do. God, I hope I don't let her down.

I'm tired and I'm hurting, but I know that the power is still there. I can feel it like a hot ball of magic wedged between my heart and my lungs. I just need to be able to get it up and out of me ... just enough to show that Indira is off limits to Godfrey now, that I can protect her.

The leather satchel slung over his shoulder is heavy. I try to pick it up, but it's too much, and he's not carrying anything else. I look quickly to Indira, to see if she might be holding anything I could use, but her bag is too heavy too. There's nothing else around us but shrubbery rooted into the ground and litter. What am I doing to do, pelt him with cola cans, crisp packets and fallen leaves?

But there is something else, something that scares me even as I'm considering it: Godfrey himself. I feel him out, and test his weight. He's far too heavy of course, but his hands aren't. Those hands, that only an hour ago were pummelling me and making me feel like the most worthless lowlife on the planet, are now mine. The pulpy feel of his skin, and each of his fingers like sticks that I can twist, so tempting... but I hold back. I don't want to hurt him, not yet and not like this. I just want to frighten him.

He's trying to move his hands to throw a punch, but I'm holding them fast.

'What the hell is this?' Godfrey yells, the force of his voice enough of a shock for me to lose it slightly, and he staggers backwards.

'He's got powers, he's a Vigil!' Indira exclaims, and her words make me stronger.

My own right arm extended to help me focus the power, I hold on to Godfrey. He tries to wrench away, then to push forward, but I've got him. It's taking everything I have, and my chest heaves with the force of my breathing, which is not in the least bit kind on my ribs, but I want him to be scared. I want him to be terrified.

'What are you doing? Let me go!' he's calling.

'Are... you going... to leave her... alone?' I say darkly on the out-breaths.

'I'll go! I'll go!' he says, and because I've never heard his voice that way – so shrill – I release him.

As I'm doubling over with exhaustion and pain (the waves of it are causing the bile to rise in my throat, and I get a flash of horror as I think about being sick while wearing the mask), Godfrey is unleashed and backs away. He doesn't go far. I can tell this, even though my eyes are closed and I'm bent over towards the ground, because I can see him in my head. Indira is worryingly silent, holding herself back, scared.

But Godfrey isn't finished. Not yet. It must be seeing me weak that gives him the burst of inspiration: he comes forward, brings a fist back and takes aim at my head. I see it all, even though I'm not looking directly at him. His eyes are on fire, and his upper lip is curled into a snarl. But however determined he is to strike me right now, it's nothing compared to my determination to not be hit. Not again, and not by him. I'm not going to let him or his friends ever get near me again, I swear.

So just as he's about to bring that fist down on me, I grab at it with my mind, and I can't help the agonised roar I give out as I force back and twist. His blow never lands, but there is an audible crunch. I don't know what bone it is, or how serious, but I know that I've done damage.

'WHAT THE HELL?!' he cries out in agony. 'WHAT DID YOU DO?'

Indira doesn't say anything. She's scared. Even though I'm not looking at her, I can tell. I can *feel* it. Floating a few hockey sticks is not the same as breaking bones, and I wonder if, without meaning to, I've crossed some horrible line. *But he came for me*, I want to explain. *I didn't want to hurt him, but what choice did he leave me? I'm not the same as him. Please don't think I'm the same as him.*

'Just go,' Indira orders him.

'But my hand?! What the hell has he done to my hand?!' Godfrey exclaims.

'I don't care. Go inside, go find a teacher. I don't care, just go!'

Amazingly, he does.

'Are you OK?' She's next to me now, her soft hand gentle on my back.

'I'm fine,' I manage to growl. I'm not fine. Everything feels hot. It's like my heart and lungs are on fire.

'Thank you for that, and sorry about him. Godfrey is a jerk. I can't believe I was going out with him.'

What? She was actually going out with him? When? If I wasn't feeling nauseous before, I definitely am now.

'Can I help you at all? Is there anything I can do? I don't even know who you are. Will you tell me?'

I stagger forward, aiming for one of the pillars of the school gate. I need to lean on something before I fall over.

'Wait here, OK? I'm going to go and get help. Promise me that you won't leave!'

She's gone, and as soon as she disappears back into the school building, I go too, in the opposite direction. I look around, scanning for anyone who might have noticed what was going on, but there's nobody. Everyone has left the main driveway now and gone home. There's

116

a strange car parked nearby – strange only because all the windows appear to be darkened and I can't see inside, but then I figure that's probably just a hilariously wealthy kid's hilariously wealthy ride. I don't go back for my bag – I don't dare risk it in case Indira comes back out and sees me – and it's hidden behind a pillar anyway so will most likely still be there tomorrow morning. The most important things, my keys and phone, are in my pockets anyway, and luckily my hoodie is baggy enough that I can hide the mask under it without it looking too conspicuous. I use my hands to straighten out my hair and start to make for the bus stop to take me home. I don't look behind me to see if Godfrey or Indira have emerged again.

Except that I don't get there.

I'm not even out of sight of the school when I realise that the car is following me. The black one, all the windows darkened so I can't see who's inside. I can't even see who's driving. Even when I try and concentrate my mind really hard, I find that although I can see all around the car, I can't see through tinted glass. The first thing that occurs to me is that it's somebody who saw what I did. I don't ever remember Godfrey having bodyguards or minders before, but seeing that his dad is a somewhat important MP, it wouldn't surprise me if he did. I pretend that I don't know that I'm being tailed. I pretend that I haven't noticed the car is crawling along just behind me, never getting too far ahead but never stopping. I wonder if it's possible for my heart to explode with stress. Because this is all I need; after being pummelled and then using every last ounce of strength to protect Indira, I've got no more fight in me.

Presuming the worst, that someone has seen me and seen what I can do, I turn into a side lane that serves as an access road to the back of the Gatford playing fields. Just as I suspected, the car follows me. When I stop, the car stops, and a woman gets out from the passenger side. She's all straight lines and sharp angles in a black trouser suit, hair tied back sleekly away from her face and her expression obscured by neat dark glasses.

'Joseph Wilkes?' the woman asks.

Are they the police? They don't look like police, and she's not flashing a badge at me. Maybe she is part of the 'Godfrey Protection Squad', in which case I'm doomed. I think that maybe I should be throwing my arms up in surrender, but my sides are too sore. So instead I find the strength to take one more deep breath and let my shoulders slump forward so that she knows that I've given up.

'Are you Joseph Wilkes?' the woman says again.

'What do you want?' I ask.

'I need you to come with me.'

'Are you the police?'

'No.'

'Then who are you?'

'We're the Vigils.'

OK – what? Seriously?

I've been picked on and made the butt of jokes often enough not to take this at face value. I'm immediately suspicious. But this lady certainly looks the part...and the car does too. Besides which, Eddie is the only person who knows about me and I don't think he'd set up an elaborate hoax like this.

'Am I in trouble?' I test.

'No...but after that little stunt back there? You're cutting it fine.' The woman's voice is low, but not menacing. If anything, I'd say that she's mildly amused.

She closes the space between us, the car keeping its distance.

'We have ways of tracking new talent. You think that you're all alone, but really you're not. Sometimes we wait to see how new powers progress, but it looks as if yours are already causing quite the commotion. As it turns out, seems like we got here in the nick of time. So, you're coming in to meet the team.'

'This is a joke, right?' Because I can't see any of this being remotely real.

'Was breaking a boy's hand with the power of your mind a joke?' Fair enough. And I'm freaked that she already knows the diagnosis on Godfrey's hand.

'So what happens now?'

119

'We take you to London, to our headquarters, get you registered.'

'Registered?' I'm still not sure about this. But I'm also not sure whether the rule about not getting into cars with strangers applies in situations like this.

'It'll all be explained once we get there.'

'And if I don't want to go with you? What if I just want to go home and forget about all of this?'

The lady takes off her sunglasses and puts them into the breast pocket of her jacket. Underneath, her eyes are ice bright and serious. She's looking straight at me, practically unblinking.

'We can do this in one of two ways. The hard, or the easy. I'd prefer the latter. And, from what I gather, you've already been put through the wringer today. Let's keep this simple, shall we? No powers, and no drama. You come with us right now, and everything will be fine.'

I gulp. Isn't this what I always wanted? Someone to finally see that I'm special? That I'm worthwhile? And now that it's here, right in front of me, why am I resisting? Maybe this is too good to be true. To be swept away by a mysterious lady in a dead-cool car, be taken straight to the headquarters of the Vigils no less, this is all too much. Plus I'm tired out, and beaten up, and what am I meant to say to my mum?

'Joseph, I strongly recommend that you come with me,' the lady says again, seeing that I'm wavering.

One more deep breath and I nod. It's started. It's time to go.

'So do you have powers?' I ask Agent Yellow.

It seems like a strange thing to call her, but that's what she's asked for, and her face is still deadly serious, so I'm not about to argue. Another guy is driving, and I've been told that his codename is Agent Green. To be honest, even from back here he seems a heck of a lot friendlier than Yellow. He chuckles to himself every now and again and mumbles insults to other drivers who annoy him (there are a lot). We're speeding down the motorway, and from this side of the darkened windows, all the other cars are just blurs of fuzzy light against the setting spring sun.

She sighs before replying: 'Unless you count being very good at my job as a superpower? Then, no.'

'So how do you get to work for the Vigils? If you don't have any powers yourself, I mean?'

'Honestly? I was scouted at university, but went through years of training before I joined officially. Agent Green was in the private security sector, isn't that right, Agent Green?'

Agent Green mumbles in the affirmative and nods his head.

'So does this car have secret rocket thrusters? Or invisibility shielding? Or anything cool like that?' I ask after we pass another exit on the motorway towards London.

'Why don't you press that button and find out?' Agent Yellow goads.

'Really?' I look down at the armrest between us, which presents a flurry of buttons and indicators on a touch-screen panel.

'Sure, go for it. You can push that red one there.'

'You're serious about this?'

'Completely.'

I look down at the panel, and at the array of buttons. My hand hovers over it for some time, as my heart races in my chest. I figure that whatever the button does, it can't really be that important, otherwise I wouldn't be allowed anywhere near it, but what if it *does* do something crazy, like send the car into turbo-mode or eject me?

Finally, anxiously, I press the button.

Nothing happens.

'So...' I say, 'that button was never going to do anything. Was it?'

'It did,' Agent Yellow responds. 'It activated the seat heaters. Things should be getting nice and toasty very soon.'

Agent Green chuckles and passes a knowing smile back to his colleague through the rear-view mirror. I decide to sit back and try to relax for the rest of the journey, and not give these two any more opportunities to wind me up.

We arrive at the entrance to an office building, right in the middle of London. I wish I could say more about where exactly we are, but I've only ever been here on school trips to the dinosaur museum and the Tower, and it's not as if Mum and I can afford to go on many jollies to the capital just for the sake of it. London is an immense mystery to me. So far it all seems very grey. The sun has set behind the skyscrapers, and the city is dismal in the twilight. I feel a pang for home. A curdle in my belly tells me that I shouldn't be here. That I should be at home, fixing dinner for me and Mum and getting on with homework. When will they let me call her? Will they let me call her at all?

'Stay close, OK?' Agent Yellow instructs.

We head up some steps to the main door, where Agent Green places his finger on a reader and swipes an ID card before we're allowed in. On the inside is a security guard sitting at a desk, reading a newspaper. He nods to the agents but not to me. All I get is a good sizing-up, which feels oddly aggressive despite the silence.

As we wait in the lobby for a lift to arrive I can't help but think that something must have gone wrong somewhere. Are we in the right place? This doesn't exactly seem like an appropriate entrance for a league of top-secret superheroes. I was expecting grand entrances, body scanners and armed guards. If anything this whole set-up just reminds me of the lawyer's office near us where Mum does administration work. Unless of course that's the point. Maybe this is some kind of 'hiding in plain sight' kind of set-up. What better way to disguise one of the most important and exciting organisations in the world than by making it look profoundly boring?

'Expecting laser beams and rocket ships coming out of swimming pools?' Agent Green checks with me after seeing my face in the mirror in the lift. 'Yeah, these things are never as fun as how they seem in the movies.'

'So, will I get to meet Deep Blue? Or Hayley Divine?' I ask as the lift pings upwards.

'Not this evening, maybe later,' Agent Yellow replies. 'We keep all the fun stuff below ground. Let's just say that today has more of an admin-type theme.'

We arrive at the fourth floor. Again I'm mildly unimpressed by the scope of this building. It all feels so tragically mundane. I want cloud-busting skyscrapers and glass lifts that soar to tremendous heights. But then I remind myself that all this must just be a very clever disguise. That the Vigils can't have anything that obvious; otherwise everybody would know where they are and how to find them. Boring works great as a camouflage, as I well know.

When the lift doors open there's a girl waiting for us. She's short, and weirdly young (no older than eighteen, surely?) and despite the fact that it's not even that cold, she has a huge rainbow-striped chunky scarf wrapped around her tiny neck. She's so small that despite the number of times it's wound around her, the end still trails nearly to the floor. But she's smiling, and she seems a heck of a lot less intimidating than Agents Yellow and Green, so I smile back and extend a hand.

'Hello, Joseph,' she says, taking my hand and shaking it happily. 'I'm really pleased to meet you. Welcome to The Strand. My name is Louise Kirby.'

10

'Sorry about all the duplicate stuff you have to fill in. We used to have this guy who looked after all the photocopying duties, but it didn't really work out, and we haven't had a chance to replace him yet.'

Louise is being really nice to me, sweet and understanding, despite the amount of work she's having me do. Every time I complete one form, it seems like another two appear in its place. Nondisclosure agreements, medical forms, insurance forms . . . if you can think of a form, there's a high chance that I've filled it in already or am about to.

'I thought everything here would be hi-tech and computerised,' I say, looking around the beige cubby where she has me working. I keep hoping for a glimpse of someone wearing brightly coloured Lycra, but so far there's been nothing. Just people in suits, all looking bored and busy.

'Oh, it is. A lot of the stuff you're filling in will be digitally sorted and archived. But there are some things that are better left on paper. I mean, I know there's been a lot in the news lately about all the documents that were lost in the Ditko Finance building fire, but trust me, cyberattacks are the absolute worst to clean up after. And you wouldn't believe the number of freaks out there with super-cybernetic powers. This way is safer, all things considered.'

It kind of feels like I've just been given a job despite not having had the interview, and there are brief moments when my heart jumps and I wonder if all this is legit or whether I'm getting myself in over my head. While she does some paperwork of her own, Louise lets me watch the Vigil welcome video, which restores my faith somewhat. It's mostly got the American Vigils in it, and Solar is the star, but I get a warm tingle when I think they're never going to be that distant from me again, and that I get to be one of them now!

When the clip finishes I look at my watch; we left Gatford at four and it's now dark outside. I must ask to phone my mum soon. She's going to freak out if she gets home from work and I'm not there.

'You'll stay here overnight, we have guest rooms. And tomorrow we've got a packed schedule of testing to do. Once we've finished here, you can go and get some rest. You'll need it.'

'What about school? What about my mum?'

'Oh, don't worry, it'll all be taken care of. You don't think a top-secret facility like this gets by without some sort of backup plan or cover-up scheme, do you? Besides which, it's my job to deal with things like that, and I'm pretty good at what I do.'

'Aren't you a little young to be working for the Vigils?' I try and ask it without sounding condescending in any way, because it's quite obvious that Louise is very capable of doing what she is doing. But I just can't believe how young she appears to be. Maybe youth is her superpower? Maybe she's ageing in reverse and really she's ninety-two?

'I'm only here part-time, some evenings and weekends,' she reveals. 'I've got my A levels coming up in a few months.'

'You're still in school?' Now I'm wondering if her dad is Quantum, or maybe Oria is her aunt? Why would she be here otherwise?

'I am. And I'll be going to university in the autumn. I'm really hoping I get into Kings or UCL, because then I'll be able to keep working here in my spare time.'

'How the heck do you go about getting a part-time job with the Vigils?'

'I have some good friends in high places...'

She lets the sentence whisper away, and I get the distinct impression that she isn't going to reveal anything more. I wonder if it's because she doesn't want to, or because she's not allowed to.

'How did you even know about me?' I try. She can't *not* tell me this.

'We employ people whose job it is to find you guys out. They're known as Visionaries.'

'Like psychics?'

'A little like that. Being "psychic" covers a broad range of possible powers, and it takes a lot of training before someone is reliable enough to be used as a Visionary.'

'Cool.'

I ponder it for a moment. The thought of someone seeing me in their dreams or visions is a little weird.

Finally, after what feels like hours of documenting every aspect of my life on paper, Louise brings out what first appears to be a normal smartphone.

'Now for the biometric data...' she trills.

As well as height and weight, she gives me a retinal scan, takes my fingerprints and swabs my mouth for DNA. This all seems frighteningly thorough. She notices all my injuries, but for some reason doesn't seem to be that concerned about them, apart from offering me some painkillers, which I turn down, because honestly, despite the beating I've taken, I don't feel nearly as bad as I think I should. Maybe it's endorphins or adrenaline or something. Except that now the adrenaline is starting to run dry...

She chuckles when I fight to stifle a yawn.

'Don't you get tired?' I ask her. 'Is that what your superpower is?'

129

'Oh, I don't have a power,' Louise replies, still smiling brightly at my obviously overtired state. 'But I like keeping busy. And I have perfected the art of multitasking. Once I've finished with you here, it's back to my digs and another couple of hours of reading.'

'Don't you ever burn out?'

'Oh, I don't do burning of any sort. I leave that to my friend...'

It's another of those moments where I feel desperate to ask her more, but again it doesn't feel right to. Plus I'm seriously tired. It's the kind of tiredness that makes me think that even getting out from this chair would require a force of effort too far. I can really feel the aching again; it's like I've been run over by a truck. If I breathe too deeply my lungs burn against my bruised ribs, and bruise splotches have begun to appear all over my upper arms and legs. Is it too late to ask for those painkillers after all?

'Agent Yellow will take you to your room now. Get some rest, and we'll see you tomorrow, OK?'

She doesn't have to say that twice. My joints click and groan as Agent Yellow appears at the side of the cubby and indicates for me to follow her.

'You need anything to eat?' she asks. 'It's late, but you might still be able to get something at the canteen.'

'I think I just need sleep,' I yawn back at her. It's clear that she doesn't find my tiredness endearing.

She hands me a nondescript carrier bag containing my mask, which I must have left in the car, and it makes me feel a little embarrassed because she's probably used to seeing all these hi-tech suits and costumes, not stupid sports gear.

I'm led to the lift, and then we travel down a few levels – I'm pretty sure that we only went four floors up, so I guess we're going underground. But I'm far too exhausted to even question it. They could be leading me to a torture chamber for all I know, and I wouldn't even complain, as long as there was the chance to lie down and close my eyes.

'This'll be your room for the night.' Agent Yellow swipes a card down a reader at the side of the door and it opens, revealing a basic but not too shabby bedroom. 'If you need anything, just pick up the phone. Otherwise, we'll come and get you in the morning.'

As soon as the door is closed behind me I stagger a few steps forward then let myself collapse on the bed. Then I groan at the pain as my chest impacts on the mattress. As I turn on my back and wait for the bruises to stop moaning, I realise that there is no window in here. It's like a cabin deep in the belly of a ship. There is a camera in the room though – it's mounted just above the door, and there's a long mirror stretching across one wall. *Is this some sort of prison cell?* I wonder as I kick off my shoes. I'm pretty sure from my expert recollection of binge-watched crime-procedural dramas that mirrors like that are indicative of two-way glass, and that someone is probably on the other side right now, watching and studying me. Well, they can study me all they like. As long as I'm allowed to sleep, I don't care what they do.

It does occur to me that technically I've been kidnapped, and technically they're keeping me here in this room like a prisoner, but this is definitely the Vigil headquarters. Didn't I see all the Vigil branded mugs and stationery in the office upstairs? Didn't Louise make me watch that cheesy introduction video? Every Vigil, even that girl Vega, must have gone through exactly the same experience as me, and if anyone is going to do things properly, then surely it would be the Vigils?

I barely manage to clamber out of my school uniform before the pull of the pillow swallows me up and the world drains away to blissful black.

The phone is ringing. At first it seems part of the dream I'm having, which is all abstract and dark, so I try to run away from it, or at least absorb the sound into everything else that is happening in my head. But it gets louder and more insistent as I surface from the darkness and back into the real world.

I sit up on the bed for a good few moments, the phone still ringing, as I get my bearings. I must have fallen asleep with the light on, still in most of my clothes. Without any windows to let me gauge the time of day, I start to wonder if in fact no time has passed at all. Maybe it's been mere minutes since I was deposited here; there's no way to tell.

Leaning over to the bedside table, I answer the phone.

'Hello?' My throat is parched, my voice hoarse.

'There are clothes in the cupboard.' It's Agent Yellow. 'Get dressed, and you'll be collected in ten minutes.'

I wonder if all superheroes are treated this way. Did Deep Blue get spirited away here one evening when he was a teenager? Who else has spent time in this very room? They aren't exactly going out of their way to make me feel special, but then I guess I'm not all that special if every other UK Vigil has come through here too.

In the cupboard are sports clothes. I sound a grumble of despair. Jogging bottoms, a T-shirt and trainers all in my size, and all a dark off-black. I don't have a good feeling about this. Sports clothes tend to mean only one thing: sports.

Agent Yellow knocks on my door just as I'm about to tie my shoelaces and gives me a withering look when she sees that they're still undone. She looks just the same as yesterday, only adding to my suspicion that the amount of sleep I've had totals mere minutes instead of hours. I crave daylight, or a clock, or something. My phone ran out of battery while I was filling out all the forms with Louise, and I don't make a habit of carrying my charger around

133

with me, so I've got no way to tell the time. It's all a little befuddling.

'Where are we going?' I ask as we start down one of the long corridors.

'First things first: breakfast.'

We take the lift up a couple levels (but still underground according to my crude and mostly brain-dead calculations) and when we emerge I'm shocked by the sight of people. Actual, real people, all heading hurriedly to a room at the end of yet another long corridor. I know what's coming before we get there, as the smells hit me the moment the lift doors open. Fresh, warm bread, and cooked eggs and bacon, and the sound of clinking mugs and cutlery. I've only had a breakfast like this once before, when we went to a hotel on the Isle of Wight, back when mum and dad were still trying to make a go of it. I was pretty young, but I've never forgotten the food. Mountains of sweet pastries, and cauldrons of every type of cereal you could imagine. Tapped vats of fruit juices, and the sound of percolating coffee. It's like that now. In the big Vigil canteen, made bright by white strip lights and a polished black floor ingrained with something that seems to sparkle, I'm in breakfast heaven.

'Stop drooling – you look like an idiot,' Agent Yellow berates me. 'Go get whatever you want, and I'll meet you at that table over there.' She points to a table in the furthest corner, well away from everybody else.

Used to only boring breakfasts, and having a practically empty stomach (the last time I ate was my school lunch yesterday), I pile my plate high with everything I can cram on to it, and that's before I spot the hot-food counter. At one point while I'm queuing for the fresh eggs, my stomach lets out the most embarrassing, horrifically loud growl, which makes the people standing either side of me (important and grown-up in their city suits) take a step backwards.

'Have you got enough there?' Agent Yellow says to me as I sit down. I get the impression that she's not a morning person. All she has in front of her is a large mug of black coffee.

But I don't care how horrified she is by the vast quantity of food I have in front of me. I'm a growing lad, and I happily pack the food away as if I've never seen food before in my life, switching between mouthfuls of bacon and hash browns to sweet tinned fruit and back again. I just wish I had more hands so that I could cram it all in more quickly.

Agent Yellow checks her watch a number of times as I finish up, sighing impatiently before announcing that it's time to go.

I want to protest (I was hoping for another run at the pastries counter), but the look she gives me suggests that her coffee hasn't quite kicked in yet, and that I don't want to be messing with her at this time of the morning.

She takes me first back up to the office where I was form-filling last night. Apparently there's more that needs to be done. Louise isn't here, but I'm welcomed by a woman called Somnia, who teeters about on kitten-heeled feet that look far too small for her apple-round body. She gives me yet another stack of paperwork that apparently needs to be completed.

After about an hour, Agent Yellow, my reluctant babysitter, informs me that it's time to go. When I ask her where, she doesn't answer. Home? What has Louise said to Mum, or the school, about where I've been? Will Eddie believe me when I tell him that I've been at Vigil headquarters?

We're back underground, in a bunker of a room that seems part science lab, part gym. When I see all the sports equipment my breakfast threatens to repeat on me. I turn to Agent Yellow, to protest or tell her that I want to go home now, but she vanishes quickly, leaving me alone with a man in a white lab coat. Isn't there some way I can skip this bit?

'So you're Joseph Wilkes,' the man says. 'I'm Doctor Starr, and today we're going to be putting you to the test!'

I don't like how excited he seems to be at the prospect of testing me. He's actually bouncing around on the balls of his feet.

'So how do you feel this morning, Joseph?' Dr Starr continues.

'I'm fine,' I reply, nervously scratching my head.

'I have it down here that you came in to us quite badly injured yesterday. Is that still the case?'

What does he mean? Is what still the case? I startle when I realise that nothing hurts. I roll my shoulders back, and they move with ease. I put my hands to my ribcage, applying pressure and waiting for the ache of pain, but there's nothing. Well, not entirely nothing, there's definitely something there, but it's more a memory of pain than the real thing. There's a tall mirror on the wall, and I lift up my top to have a look at the skin underneath. Blotchy and red, yes, but not the patchwork of bruises I was expecting.

'This is impossible! I was beaten up yesterday, and everything hurt. How come there's almost nothing there?' I exclaim.

'It's a common side effect of being gifted. We see it a lot, an enhanced ability to heal. I don't recommend you go around testing it and, trust me, you're still mortal, but it seems that whatever it is that accelerates powers also accelerates your body's ability to heal itself. Comes in handy, should disaster strike,' Dr Starr explains.

I've got to admit, the realisation of this new ability gives me a sudden vigour. I *am* a superhero, and I *am* special. This super-healing proves it! It's hard not to get ahead of myself when I begin to imagine all the possibilities.

Dr Starr starts me on the exercise bike. Like yesterday when I was running, I find that I'm able to achieve far more than I ever could before. I manage to keep a consistent pace, my asthma a long-ago memory. Even when the doctor turns the resistance up I push through, and whenever he reaches for his pen to note something down, I get a flurry of excitement. He tests me on the treadmill and on the weights machines, each time pushing me to my absolute limit. After about an hour I'm exhausted, and completely regretting how much I had for breakfast.

'And now we test your brain!' Dr Starr enthuses.

What happens is a series of tests not too dissimilar to what I've already practised on my own and with Eddie. He gives me wooden shapes of various sizes, and I work my absolute hardest to lift them. The first item is a bead about the size of a pea, which I manage to lift up to my eye level with barely any strain. Dr Starr seems impressed. Next, he blindfolds me in order to test my mind-vision power, and asks me to do the same with various other objects, sometimes presenting three or four on the table and asking me to pick up one while specifically ignoring the others. The only problem is that I can't seem to see through the blindfold. This is embarrassing. I try and tell him that if I closed my eyes, or looked the wrong way, then I could do it. For some reason seeing beyond my own eyelids doesn't count. But cover up my eyes with something, and I can't see a thing. Dr Starr is less impressed now, and I feel bad, like I've done something horribly wrong. Is he going to let me live and train with the Vigils here in London? Does he still think I have the potential to save the world?

Then things start getting even harder, and my head starts hurting. The now familiar tension in my temples builds, so that I have to bring my fingers up to massage the pain away. I feel like I've been working too hard and I want a break, but I'm too nervous to say so. Plus, I want to impress Dr Starr. I don't want him to know that I'm tired already, especially when I've barely done anything. I'm also aware that I'm thinking far too much. I want to tell him that I'm able to do so much more when I'm pumped full of adrenaline and barely have time to think. But like this, in a sterile and clearly very safe room, my mind wanders and I overthink, and I seem to lose some of the magic. When I start struggling with a block the size of a Rubik's Cube, the doctor places a reassuring hand on my shoulder and tells me that it's time for me to rest. Finally. He has some calls to make, and then someone will come and let me know what's next.

I'm led to a lounge to wait in, decorated in the same austere colours as the rest of this basement complex but significantly more comfortable, with a deep plush sofa and a fancy kitchenette in one corner. The walls are covered with framed bright posters of the Vigils, all posing with their hands on their hips or folded imposingly over their chests. On the far wall is a familiar group promo shot from a few years ago, with all the key people lined up in their most recognisable outfits. Quantum is front and centre, flanked by Deep Blue and the Red Rose on either side, followed by all the others in the pantheon. There's Hayley Divine, and Oria, plus a load of the less well-known British heroes, like Cheat Code, and Torpedo, Dragon, Solder and Wavelength. They're all standing in front of a backdrop of the union flag, and I can't help but imagine myself there too. I picture my costume, form-fitting (I will of course have put on more muscle mass by this point), sleek grey with silver edging, with a helmet-mask fashioned after the fencing mask, in tribute to my early days.

A part of me can't believe that this is all really happening, while another part wants to stand up and yell, *OF COURSE IT'S HAPPENING.* This is all I've ever wanted deep down, to be special, and now that my time has come I can't deny anything. I've suffered years as an outcast, lonely (save for Eddie), and at the bottom of the social food chain. Well, my time as a bottom-feeder is over. This is what I was destined to be, and hadn't I always known it? Didn't Mum always tell me that I was special, and that I was going to save the both of us one day?

When Dr Starr comes back into the room, accompanied by Agent Yellow and Louise, I'm almost crying with anticipation and expectant happiness.

'Hi, Joseph,' Louise says. 'Looks like it's time to go home!'

11

'Home?' I ask. I'm not staying here to hone my skills and be inducted on to the A-team?

'Well, the whole point of yesterday and today was just to get you on the system and to see where your powers are right now. We used to have agents who went out to process this kind of thing in the field, but of late we figure that it's better to bring you in relatively early, get you onside and everything, so that you know who the good guys are.'

'And you're definitely the good guys?' I tease, trying to sound light about it, but fearing that I come across a little arrogant because I'm disappointed.

'Oh, definitely.' Louise smiles as she looks down at Dr Starr's notes. 'And then, as your powers get more developed and refined, you might get asked back in. It's different for everybody, depending on what your powers are and how strong you are. You're lucky that you're pretty small fry. No one's that concerned about you at this stage. We just needed to make sure that you're OK and that we get you registered and in the system.'

Small fry? Did she say *small fry*?

'You might get a handler – that means someone who will be your point of contact with us – and they'll answer any other questions you might have. Or, if something happens, or if you're worried about anything, then they'd be the person you'd speak to about it. Your powers are developing nicely, and that's good, but it's never a good idea to push people to do too much too soon. Eventually, when you're a bit older, then maybe you'll be given a job here as a field agent or something.'

'But what about saving people? And everything else?' I ask.

'Oh, that kind of thing only happens for a tiny proportion of gifted people. You know, the flyers and such,' explains Dr Starr. 'There are different levels, or spheres, if you will, of powers. At first I was hopeful that maybe you had something really special, what with that ability to see beyond the scope of what is considered normal. There is some psychic potential there, that's for certain. But at this point, there's no way to know if it will develop further, or if it's just a psychic blip, a side effect of all the changes that are happening right now in your brain. I know we've only done a short assessment, but I'd say based on what I've seen, for the most part you'll probably find that you end up living a really normal life. So I wouldn't worry too much about it,' he ends cheerfully.

My brain can't quite process it. I say their words over and over to myself in my head. I'm small fry. I won't have to worry too much about it...normal life...I feel like maybe they're trying to comfort me with these words, like they think I might be freaking out about having to get involved with all the big stuff, but really it's the opposite. I guess I always presumed that I was important, that somehow I would matter within the big picture. But now...all I'm thinking over and over is small fry. Small fry. *Small fry.*

'Don't look so worried,' Dr Starr says. 'One of the forms you've filled out with Louise was a psychometric test, and I can already tell you now that you're considered low risk. No megalomaniac tendencies, so I don't think anyone here is too concerned that you're going to start a quest for world domination anytime soon. You're young, and your powers are still very new. You just need practice, and time, and we'll be checking up on you periodically. It's best for you to carry on at school for now and just see how or if your powers progress any further.'

Louise adds, 'But you've seen and signed the forms, so no bringing unnecessary attention to yourself. It tends to cause a little panic down our end when things start getting public. They don't like working with anyone whose identity has been compromised.' She rolls her eyes dramatically.

'My best friend Eddie knows,' I say.

'Oh. Do you trust him?'

'Definitely. With my life.'

She gives a wistful smile. 'Well, from experience, I think it's good to have someone you can trust. But make sure he keeps your secret. For now though, I think it's pretty safe to say that as long as you keep your head down and stay out of trouble, then your life will be nice and normal. For the most part.'

'So I won't get to meet Deep Blue? Or Hayley Divine?'

'Maybe one day?' Louise offers, but I'm not sure that I believe her. 'Oh, and before Agent Yellow takes you home, you should know that your mum thinks you got a last-minute place on a GCSE History symposium in London, all expenses paid as per the terms of your scholarship.'

I feel a wave of worry when I think about Mum. Should I tell her the truth about where I've been, or is the lie safer? Am I even allowed to tell her?

'Take this bag,' Louise says. 'It contains a load of typed-up notes in case she asks you any questions. Try and have a look at it on the way home.'

'I'm not sure about lying to my mum ...' I say.

'It's up to you. You're allowed to reveal who you are to close family if you trust them to keep your secret and as long as you're aware of the consequences if they don't. We've given you the cover story if you're not ready to tell her. It's completely up to you.'

144

I must look a bit worried.

'Do you get on with your mum?'

'We're pretty close,' I reply. 'We've been through a lot together.'

'Well then, a word of advice? I'd tell her what's going on. It's best to tell them early, I think.'

'I think I might wait,' I admit.

'What for?'

'Until I can do something really cool? Until I have the chance to make life better for us? She works two jobs so that I can afford to go to my school – and that's despite the scholarship – and I think I thought that maybe I could save her.'

'Well, who knows what the future has in store?'

'I thought having powers was going to be better than this ...'

'It's not all like on the telly. Those people you see on the news, flying here and there and saving people's lives? They're real people too. And they have real problems. Everything you worry about doesn't magically get better when you discover you have powers – if anything, it can get a lot worse.'

I wonder how she got to be so sensible when she's only a couple of years older than me.

Agent Yellow guides me out to the lobby, where Agent Green is waiting, chatting with the guy on the reception desk.

'Aww...don't look so glum,' Agent Green says to me. 'You're not the one on babysitting duty.'

'So that's it? You guys take me home and I just have to pretend that nothing's happened?' I ask.

'Pretty much.' Agent Yellow sighs, opening the door ahead of me and holding it back for us.

The car journey home is another non-event. This time Agent Yellow sits up front in the passenger seat with her colleague instead of with me in the back, but I don't feel like I'm being chauffeured, I feel like I'm just some naughty brat that the grown-ups have become tired with.

It's a dark, dismal day. Even though it's not quite sunset yet, most cars have their lights on, and I watch them streaking past as we sail along the motorway, blurs of reds, yellows and whites that reflect up from the wet tarmac and refract through the littering of raindrops on the window. If I let my eyes lose focus then they blur further into an urban rainbow, a gritty, fast swirl of street lights, brake lights and front beams. It's hypnotising. As the car keeps a steady speed the smudges of light become a metronome, with other cars zooming past us like dull drumbeats. I let my head rest back against the seat – I don't even know where we are – and I think about everything that isn't mine.

I convince the agents to go via the school so that I can run and pick up my backpack from behind the main entrance. I pray that it's still there and hasn't been found

146

by the caretaker or something; good news is that it is, but the bad is that it's wet through thanks to this horrible weather. I run back to the car using my bag as a crude umbrella, and we speed away.

Mum is out at work and I have the flat to myself. I place all the books and stuff in my bag on various radiators so that they can dry out and then flop down on my bed, lying at an awkward angle so that I can get my phone charged while still being able to look at it. There's a voicemail from my mum, with her sounding very annoyed that I forgot to tell her about visiting London and asking whether I've packed spare underwear, and then a few messages from Eddie asking if I'm OK because I'm not in school today.

Then there's another message, one that I wasn't expecting. It's a private message through one of those sites that everyone in the school is connected to, one that I don't use that often because Eddie's the only person from school I tend to have any communication with, so it stuns me for a moment, and then I bring the phone close to my face so that I can read it properly. It's from Indira:

Heard that you're a history geek? Need some help on the new project and someone said you might be the one to talk to. Can we discuss after school tomorrow?

When did she send it? Three hours ago. During last break. The story about me going to this random symposium must have reached school somehow. Should I reply straight away, or should I play it cool and bring it up

147

casually when I go back into school tomorrow? I feel like the universe is giving me a sweet gift to make up from the weird disappointment of this morning. So I won't get to be a proper Vigil just like that, but that's OK so long as there's a chance in this life that I'll be able to get closer to Indira. If I can just make her see who I really am, then surely it'll all be worth it?

The next morning Mum's off to work before I even get up but she's left a note saying I need to get better at communicating with her. She's referring to my not telling her about the history thing, but it makes me think more about what Louise said about telling Mum my secret soon. But I'm not ready to. The two of us have had enough trouble to deal with in the past. I'm not ready to give Mum more to worry about unless I have to.

The day drags on and I focus on my meeting with Indira, avoiding thinking about the fact that I'm not about to be a Vigil anytime soon. Earlier in maths I was staring so intently at the clock that I accidentally moved the minute hand forward five whole minutes. I didn't mean to; it just happened. But then I spent the whole last quarter of the lesson trying to get it back again. I just can't stop thinking about the end of the day, and seeing Indira. Being close to her, and with no one else around. *This'll be it*, I think. *This will make up for yesterday's colossal let-down.*

I try and ignore all the gossip about Godfrey's hand. He had the day off yesterday to get it all bandaged and plastered up at the hospital, and is back today looking angry and miserable. Nobody seems to know what really happened, which means that he hasn't told anyone. The minutes and seconds of the day ebb away until finally, mercifully, the final bell rings. I can't get out quickly enough. But every single person who could possibly be in my way manages to get in front of me, walking far too slowly, and stopping to look at their phones and chat. Don't they know that I have somewhere to be? That someone is waiting for me?

We've arranged to meet in the library, and as it turns out I get there before her. But this is good. It means that I can settle and be calm instead of arriving in a flustered, red-faced panic. I lay out the history textbook and a notebook from my bag, but ten minutes after the final bell has rung, Indira is still not here, and my insides clench, wondering whether this is all some big wind-up.

I'm not the only one here. There seem to be a lot of kids hanging out, using the room as study space or just chatting. There are quite a few from the year above me, revising for their GCSEs. The ones who want quiet are up on the mezzanine, where there's usually a teacher stationed, marking homework or lesson planning while supervising. Not that we need that much supervision. Let's just say that the kids who come to hang out in the library aren't exactly the wild sort. Those kids are all outside in the late-afternoon sunshine, tearing into each other on the rugby field or getting as far away from school as possible.

When Indira finally turns up – just when I had given up all hope that she would – I've completely doodled over the first free page in my notepad. I tear the page out and scrunch it into a little ball, getting rid of it just in time.

'Sorry I'm late!' Indira says, taking the seat opposite me.

For a moment I'm struck dumb, wondering what on earth I'm meant to say. This is nearly too much, and almost in time with the rate that my heart is beating, my pen starts to rattle on the tabletop. Nothing too obvious, but a gentle tapping, as though the table was being shaken beneath it. I move my hand over it as soon as I realise what's happening, which is just in time.

'I was chatting and lost track of the time,' Indira says by way of explanation as she gets her books out. She doesn't seem happy. In fact she seems rather agitated, so I immediately think that it's something about me, that I'm the one making her angry somehow.

'Are you OK?' I feel like I'm testing the water with my big toe, nervous and ready to jump out if it's too hot.

She looks at me with serious eyes, as if trying to work out whether I'm the right person to talk to. Then she sits down in a huff.

'No, not really.'

'Anything I can help with – or is it just the history coursework?'

'It's Godfrey, isn't it?' she says.

'Godfrey?' I act like I'm surprised.

'Yes. Godfrey. Sometimes I don't even know what I ever saw in him. It's really difficult, you know?'

I don't know. But if I needed any more reasons to absolutely hate Godfrey Chappell, I now have another.

'Has he done something?' I ask.

Another audible sigh, followed by her dramatically resting her head on her folded arms.

'I don't even know if I should be telling you this,' she mumbles from where she's hidden her face. Then she looks straight at me: 'But then, it's not as if you're going to go around telling people, are you? No offence, but it's not like you're known for gossip, and if I told one of my girlfriends, it would end up all around the school in seconds. So promise me this goes no further.'

I motion that my lips are sealed.

'So this Godfrey thing – oh god, I seriously can't believe that I'm telling you this – well, it was going all right for a while. Nothing serious, but nice, you know? And then something happened. I met someone, and this is going to sound absolutely crazy, but I don't even know who this someone really is, and yet I can't stop thinking about him. I think that maybe, quite possibly, I might be *in love* with him.'

151

'You're in love with Godfrey?' I test, slowly.

'No, silly, with this other person. This mystery guy.' Indira blushes. 'I don't even know who he really is, can you believe it? But I think he might be a Vigil. He was wearing a mask. I literally bumped into him after school the other day, and then you know about Godfrey's hand?'

I nod to let her know that I do.

'Well, he did that. He did it for me. He was standing up for me because Godders was being an absolute arse.'

'Right...' My mouth is so dry that it's hard to get the words out. 'And you're in love with him? This Vigil guy?'

'I know, it's ridiculous, right? I don't even know who he is! But he was, like, defending my honour. I'm sure of it.'

I feel my face redden and the pen trapped under my hand begins to rattle again. 'So why was Godfrey hassling you in the first place?'

'It's all about him wanting more from me, and these pictures I sent him – that's a whole other story – and then the masked man showed up at just the right moment, and defended me, like a real Vigil! So of course I told Godfrey that I had met him before...'

'You told Godfrey what?'

'I told Godfrey that I had met him before, in the mask and everything, and Godfrey went crazy! I mean, he's on a bunch of drugs because his hand is really messed up, but he's still not over it. That's the real reason why I was

152

late here; we were arguing about it. I want him to lay off and let this masked guy do his thing, to see what happens, but Godfrey has got his heart set on exposing him or something. He's been saying that his hand got broken in an accident because he doesn't want anyone to know that he lost a fight, but now that he thinks that there's something going on with me and him, Godfrey is livid.'

'Right...'

'It's, like, become this whole vendetta thing. Plus of course he has all this extra energy because he can't play the match against Queen's any more.'

'Godfrey's off the rugby team?'

'Well, he can't exactly play with a broken hand, can he? Oh, and did I tell you what this masked guy's power is? He can move things with his mind! Can you believe it? A real Vigil, who possibly goes to Gatford! I've been so desperate to talk about all of this, you know? But I can't tell my friends, because I sound like a crazy person. I mean, we've not even spoken, and I have no idea who he is. You don't think I'm crazy, do you?'

'No...' I say carefully. 'But, umm...how exactly did Godfrey say that he was going to get his revenge?'

'He's got this plan to expose the masked man in front of the whole school, once he's figured out who he is. We figure that he must be a Gatford boy, because both times I've seen him, it's been here. Do you think that he might be a sixth-former? He's not all that tall, probably about your height... but don't you think that this is all really exciting?'

'And you're in love with him?' I need to hear it again, just one more time.

'Love's a funny word, you know? But the truth is that I can't stop thinking about him.'

I could tell her. I could tell her right now. I could lean in just a tiny bit closer and whisper it into her ear. What would she do? What would she say? I could prove it to her too, with my pen or something else. I'd try to amaze her, to make this all magical, to make the world dance right in front of her eyes. But... I already have a strong suspicion that Indira could never keep it a secret. And the Vigils have warned me not to draw attention to myself. She might go and call Godfrey with the news, and then I'd be dead. *Dead* dead.

'You're really sweet, you know? It's actually nice talking to you. You're a good listener. Has anyone ever told you that?'

'We should get on with some work,' I suggest, fighting the blush and forcing down the thumping of my heart, leaning back a little in my seat so that I'm not so close to her. 'So what was it you needed help with?'

I open up the textbook, and she opens hers to the same page.

'It's the Mussolini assignment,' she says. 'I don't really

get what we're supposed to do and, I find it all totally boring.'

I begin to talk to her about Italy, about Mussolini.

'This is so hard . . .' Indira moans. It really isn't – it's just reading and understanding, but I don't say that. Instead I try to explain it in a different, simpler way.

'I honestly think I have too much happening in my brain. It's all getting mushed up.'

Then her phone vibrates on the table. I will myself not to use my mind-eyes to see the name on the screen.

'I'll just be a moment, OK?' She answers it and gives me a sad little wave before she takes it out of the library to be able to talk properly.

I sit back and look around me at all the shelves of books, then start doodling big bold squares and random polygons: loud stars and lopsided triangles. I should tell her about me. I really want to tell her. Maybe it would ease her stress levels if she knew. But what would happen next? Just because she's supposedly in love with the masked guy, doesn't mean that she'll fall in love with me, does it? Who exactly does she imagine is under the mask?

Indira comes rushing back into the room, still clutching her phone to her ear, holding her hand over it so that the person on the other end can't hear what she's saying.

'Look, I'm really sorry, but something's come up,' she says to me.

'OK. We can rearrange?' I offer.

'I'm not sure . . . But listen, I know that you helped out Tessa Hopkins last term with her project work. I mean, that's why they call you Wilco, isn't it?' I don't like where this is going at all. 'I wouldn't normally ask, and I've never done this before, I promise, but I've really got to take this call . . .'

'You want me to do your homework for you?'

'I know, I know, I'm terrible, but there's nothing I can do about it. Just, find me a load of weblinks or something? Email them over to me and I'll have a look. Or we can meet up before class and you can tell me lots of clever things in case Mr Jones asks me about it?'

'Are you sure . . . ?'

'You'd be doing me a huge favour.' Her eyes slide towards her phone, as if there's someone very important on the other end.

'Sure,' I relent. Because I'm Wilco. And I will always comply.

'Oh, thank you, Wilco! Thank you so much, I owe you big time!' She comes around the table and hugs me and, while she's right there, plants a feather kiss on my cheek, but I'm not as excited about it as I would have thought I should be. I feel cold, and annoyed. I give her a light pat on the back as she grips me close, wishing that she would just go already so that I can get on with my moping.

After she's gathered up her things and left, I feel broken and grumpy. I consider texting Eddie, asking where he is, but then I think that he must be busy somewhere wooing Kesia, and I wouldn't want to do to him what whoever-it-was just did to me.

I'm tapping my pen on the table, and I let out a gigantic sigh so loud that some of the kids at the next table turn to look at me. So I pack up my things, shrug my rucksack on to my back and take myself home.

12

What was merely the disappointing news that Godfrey couldn't take part in the rugby because of an injury has turned into explosive gossip. Someone has leaked the truth about how he hurt his hand. My bet would be on Indira telling one of her girlfriends, but however it got out there, now it seems like the whole school is talking about the mysterious masked man who attacked Godfrey.

One group of kids I pass in the quad are saying things like: 'He's a hero! Finally Godfrey got what he deserved!'

While just further along the same path I hear some others say: 'He's trying to sabotage the game! The man is a menace to our school!'

It's weird. Sometimes I feel like I should be revelling in this, while at other times I feel like I just want to run and hide under a rock until all this trouble goes away. Godfrey's blowing this all out of proportion, especially as he's completely failed to mention that he was about to mess the masked guy up, and that the hand breakage was a last-resort method of self-defence. To listen to one of

Godfrey's fans tell the story, I pretty much tortured the guy for no reason whatsoever. It takes a lot of self-control not to butt in and set things straight.

Then there's the scrutiny that Indira is facing. Since this has all blown up she hasn't been shy to let everybody know her part in the story. Except she's painting it as some grand chivalric fight for her honour, which is a bit of an exaggeration too. I wish she would tell the truth about what really happened, but she doesn't seem to want to let everyone know that Godfrey is a bully. I guess that Godfrey is too powerful for that, plus her own version of events sounds more romantic anyway.

But I hear what they say about her too: 'I bet she's making all this up for attention,' and 'She thinks she's so special.' So much for her most-popular-girl-in-the-school status. None of this is nice to hear, and it sucks that I can't defend her.

What results is a couple of days of keeping my head firmly down and staying as far away from Godfrey as humanly possible. I don't risk wearing the mask again. The Vigils asked me to keep a low profile, and I want to prove that I can be reliable, so I put the mask in a plastic bag and try to stuff it in my locker, but it won't fit. We only have those small lockers barely big enough for a single schoolbag, and after considering whether or not it would be safe to keep the mask in my room (the answer is no: too many questions to answer if Mum found it), I

159

bundle the bag in the space above the lockers. There's all sorts of sports crap stowed up there, and an extra bag stuffed with a fencing mask surely won't be out of place.

'It'll all blow over eventually,' Eddie says. I had to tell him the truth about what happened after PE, and while Eddie would never condone violence of any sort, he understands that I wasn't left with much of a choice.

Not that we can talk about it too much, because wherever we go Kesia is still following.

'Have you even asked her out yet?' I ask him during biology, one of the few classes we have together but without her.

'I'm waiting for the right time,' Eddie admits. Surely there must be at least twelve 'right times' a day, because she seems to be *everywhere*. 'Want to come to my house after school tonight? We can practise your powers in the garden or something?'

'I'm not sure...' I say, my words trailing off. What's the point of practising? What's the point of any of it? I am just *small fry* after all. I know I should have told Eddie about going to the Vigil headquarters when I told him about the fight with Godfrey, but the thought makes me cringe. What am I supposed to say? They brought me in, and then they sent me away again, and made me feel like a complete idiot in between? It's too embarrassing.

So far there's been no more mention of Godfrey exposing the masked man. I'm even starting to feel hopeful that everything will soon blow over and be forgotten. It's not as if there's any way Godfrey could possibly find out, so I decide that my secret must be safe. I remember that the girl of my dreams admitted that she's in love with me, and the heaviness and anxiety finally seem to be lifting. I think about ways that I could tell her, with grand gestures and romance, and I start to understand what Eddie means when he says that he's waiting for the right time. Every time I think about going up to her and asking to have a word, it's just not right. The weather isn't warm enough, or she's just had a bad mark in history, or I've overheard one of her friends saying something I don't like about my alter ego.

It's at the end of maths on Thursday that I know something weird is happening. There's a strange vibe in school. Eddie doesn't seem to have noticed it, but I have. People are whispering and frantically checking their phones. There's a buzz building, the kind that makes me wonder if there's been a big Vigil save somewhere. Whenever there's a big disaster that involves Vigils, everyone has a tendency to go a bit mad watching the footage online and commenting in the forums afterwards. If it is a big-save scenario, then I don't want to know. I don't want anything to do with the Vigils right now; I don't want to think about how close I am to being one of them, and yet how far away.

I manage to stay away from all the gossip until

lunchtime (it's not as if I'm that in with all the various cliques to be included in their round-table discussion of events), but when I meet Eddie in the memorial garden it's quite clear that he's bursting with news. Kesia is there too (what a surprise!), eyes downcast over her heavy book and chewing on a long strand of brown hair, but she might as well be invisible as she's so quiet and uninterested. She doesn't even look up when I come along; I'm not even sure if she's heard me approach.

'What is it then?' I sigh to Eddie, who looks like he's about to explode.

'Haven't you heard?' Eddie's eyebrows stretch so high up his forehead I'm surprised they don't fly off.

'Heard what?'

'Godfrey's going to unmask the masked man! Today!' Eddie exclaims, throwing both arms wide.

I purse my lips in apprehension, aware that even though Kesia doesn't look like she's listening, there are still some things I don't want her to hear. Without giving anything away, I ask Eddie what he means. He takes out his phone and shows me the message:

Assembly hall after school! ALL WILL BE REVEALED!

'How do you know that it's about . . . you know what?' I ask. Godfrey can't possibly have sussed it out yet. How could he?

'Mate, what else could it be about? Godfrey's going to blow this whole thing wide open!'

'And you think that's a good thing?' I exclaim. I want to swear. I want to run away and vanish into a cloud where no one can see me. This is a huge disaster. I was told not to tell anyone.

'You have to go,' Eddie tells me. 'We don't even know if Godfrey has it right. And don't you need to find out?'

'But surely it's better if I'm not there, right?' I keep my voice low, glaring at him meaningfully, and trying not to say anything too obvious that could be overheard. 'I mean, he can't make me do anything if I'm not actually there.'

'Well, yes ... but ... People will notice if you're not there. You'll be conspicuous by your absence, especially if Godfrey does reveal all and gets it right.'

'How do we even know what he's going to say? This could all be one huge wind-up, or just some crazy stunt.'

Godfrey can't know anything. There's no way. Is there?

'Look, here's what you do,' Eddie says, leading me away from Kesia and talking softly. 'You go along and you listen to what he has to say. If he "outs" you, just play dumb. Wave a bit, look stupid and then all the focus will have to go back to Godfrey. He's going to look like the idiot, not you. And if he gets it wrong, then he still looks like an idiot! You can't lose!'

I pick at a nearby shrub, pulverising the leaves between my fingers until they smell sweet and get sticky.

'I don't know about this . . .' I say.

'Look at it this way: either you're there and you get to watch this entire thing blow over into nothing by the end of the day, or you're not there and everything builds and builds and you have no control over it.'

'This isn't the way it's meant to be,' I sigh, thinking about Louise, and then seeing Agent Yellow's disapproving face in my mind.

'Well, I did warn you not to mess with him,' Eddie says.

'You weren't there, I didn't have a choice. He would have smashed my head in,' I reply.

'Look, what does he even have on you anyway? How could he possibly know the truth?'

That's exactly what I think, but then I also know that Godfrey wouldn't risk making a fool out of himself unless he was sure.

I leave Eddie with Kesia in the garden and head towards my locker, where I have my textbooks for the afternoon lessons stashed. All around me I notice people buzzing about Godfrey's big reveal. Groups of girls cluster in corners, giggling and hazarding wild guesses. Boys swigging energy drinks lean against the noticeboards and howl with laughter as crazy names are thrown into the mix. I overhear one guy proclaiming that the masked man might even be Godfrey himself. I feel uneasy about all of this, and weirdly detached from it too. Because how can Godfrey possibly know anything? And what's he trying to achieve by parading his unfounded suspicions in front of the whole school?

When I reach my locker, something doesn't feel right. Something in my brain is fizzing, telling me to beware and pay close attention. I open the door slowly, as though it might be booby-trapped, and instinctively use my psychic vision to check inside before I have the door open the whole way, in case something leaps out at me. I breathe a sigh of relief when I find everything is normal.

Getting from English to the assembly hall at the end of the day feels like dragging myself through mud. I'm a deflated ball that just refuses to roll. I meet Eddie next to the Wall of Fame (a giant board where the names of all the head boys and head girls gone by reside) and I'm so nervous that I can't even speak. My insides churn and burble.

'Mate, don't worry! What could he know? It's all going to blow over and be fine, just you see!' Eddie insists.

The assembly hall is packed. Most of the school must be in here, including a few curious teachers, which means space is tight. I keep my head low, and daren't make eye contact with anyone. I'm just a regular Joe, same as everyone else here.

Eddie and I find a pocket of space to stand in and we both look around nervously. Kesia is standing nearby with some of the other new friends she's made, and Eddie gives her a goofy wave whenever she turns to look at us.

Her lips curl up into a hint of a smile in return. Maybe he's making progress?

Just like a rowdy audience in a theatre, the crowd hushes as Godfrey makes his entrance, the king of Gatford House. He gets up onstage flanked by some of his inner circle: the two Williams and another rugby boy called Scott. He takes his place at the lectern with all the demonic superiority of an ancient Roman Caesar.

'Er...hi!' he starts.

It's a surprisingly less than authoritative start, to be honest. He's nervous, something I find reassuring.

'We all know why we're here today!' Godfrey calls out over the murmuring of the crowd. I keep my head low and hope that he hasn't spotted that I'm here. 'Last week I was assaulted and my hand fractured in three places. As a result I've been ruled out of the match against Queen's next week, and quite possibly for the rest of the term. Now, I know that some of you have your theories, but I'm here today to tell you the truth. And that truth is this...' Dramatic pause. 'I was the victim of a psychic attack that afternoon, by a person with superpowers. A pupil at this school. As many of you know, I have experience of these things, thanks to the work of my father. This person has the power to move objects with his mind and should be regarded as dangerous. He has already tried to hurt me, and this sort of thing cannot be tolerated in a place like Gatford House. We cannot allow certain individuals to just run rampant with their supernatural abilities. We are all in danger!'

Expectant and thrilled silence.

'I wasn't sure at first who this person was – he was masked, and he's been careful not to be seen again. But last night I found some key evidence!' Godfrey signals to one of the Williams who delves into a familiar plastic bag and pulls out a fencing mask. My fencing mask. He hands it to Godfrey. 'This is what my attacker was wearing!'

Oh no. That explains the funny feeling I had back at my locker. The locker itself was fine, just as I left it, but I didn't register that the mess above had been cleared away. It was all empty space; I can picture it now. And my mask was in there. He must have spotted it somehow, maybe when the caretakers were clearing up? Maybe when it was on the junk pile? Why was I so careless?

The crowd shifts forward with curiosity.

'But would you believe it, the fool even had his name sewn into it!' Godfrey holds the mask up into the air, and my heart stops beating. This isn't right – I've never sewn my name into anything in my life.

'Ladies and gentlemen, the masked man is: EDWARD OLSEN!'

With a frantic gasp the crowd turns inward on itself, and quite honestly my first reaction is to wonder if this is another Olsen sibling or cousin that I haven't come across yet. It takes me an embarrassingly long moment to realise that Godfrey is talking about Eddie. *My* Eddie. The name sewn into the kit is 'Olsen' for his brother Hal, and Godfrey has presumed the rest. For some reason I turn expectantly to Eddie too, feeling the aura of shock and horror around me and expecting him to react. Which he doesn't. Not at first. And then, as being onstage in front of the whole school is pretty much his dream scenario, he pushes his glasses up his nose and offers up his trademark goofy wave and smile to the world.

Two of Godfrey's friends come forward and scoop Eddie out of the crowd. They walk him towards the stage like bodyguards, while Eddie looks around at everybody in baffled amusement. I stay where I am, waiting to see how this is all going to unfold. But already things are different to what I had expected. There's no fear, nor vitriol, nor hate. I look around, and people are smiling. They're in awe, and they're excited. To my left I even hear the beginning of some chanting: 'Eddie! Eddie! Eddie! . . .'

Eddie clambers up on the stage and stands proud and tall like all his dramatic training has taught him, before managing a tiny wave to Kesia. I look around to where she is standing. She looks straight at me. When our eyes meet, her face goes cold and serious as steel. Her features tighten and her eyes seem to shoot laser beams of intensity right at me. It makes her look older. Did Eddie tell her the truth about me already? Is she angry that I've got him into trouble?

Godfrey is clearly not expecting this reaction. His face is hot and red, and I can see his knuckles whiten with tension where he grips them tight.

While all this is happening I start to feel a little removed from myself, like I'm watching events play out on a screen in front of me, like I'm not even really here. Godfrey's trying to say something, but he's not loud enough and the chanting is spreading. Eddie is revelling in it, while I just watch, unable to do anything or take any control. This is not how it was supposed to go, for me or for Godfrey.

'Eddie! Eddie! Eddie!' the crowd continues, fists thumping the air and feet stamping on the polished wooden floor.

'Wait a minute, just wait!' Godfrey tries to contain the thrill of the crowd. He really isn't happy.

'Do something! Do something! Do something!' The crowd has moved on. They're louder now, insistent. I half expect Eddie to start tap-dancing just because he can.

I overhear conversations around me: 'Why doesn't he do anything?' and 'He'd be the coolest person in the whole school if he really did have powers...'

'I bet he's a phoney. I bet Godfrey's set this whole thing up.'

'But didn't you hear? Indira's been telling people that he's practically her boyfriend!'

'I don't care who it is... I just want to see some superpowers!'

Eddie is flailing up there. He clearly can't do anything, and is starting to look really silly, especially as each second that goes by without a demonstration of power just makes him look more foolish. This whole thing is turning into a serious joke.

I think about it: would admitting having superpowers make me the coolest person in the school? Would everyone be chanting my name instead of Eddie's? As far as I can tell, this whole meeting has not had the effect Godfrey was intending. Instead of humiliating and turning everyone against Eddie, the crowd is loving him. Could they love me like that? Are the Vigils wrong? Am I more than small fry?

'Wait,' I hear myself saying. But I'm removed. It's not really me; it's a me that's far away. 'Wait!'

I'm pushing my way through the crowd, almost to the front, and Eddie is looking at me, shaking his head.

'No!' he's saying. 'Go back!'

'It's not him.' There's that voice again. It sounds just like mine, but loud and persistent. 'He's not the one!'

Godfrey's staring down at me from the stage, his head cocked at a confused and disjointed angle. 'What the hell?' I can see his mouth muttering as I get even closer.

I'm at the front now, looking up at the stage where Eddie and Godfrey are looking back down at me, Eddie with horror and Godfrey with baffled confusion. Except that slowly, moment by moment, the confusion is

170

contorting into revelation. I use my arms to propel myself up on to the stage, and Godfrey stands back to give me room, unable to say anything as he realises the truth, why I'm standing up here.

'Joseph, mate, you don't have to do this,' Eddie hisses, coming close. 'I've got it, we can have them fooled for a bit, nobody has to know.'

'It's OK,' I say, the far-off voice sounding closer now. 'I think it's going to be OK.'

I move around so that I'm standing up in front of the crowd. The chanting has died down as people wonder what the hell I'm doing up here. I'm wondering what the hell I'm doing up here, but I'm also thinking about people chanting my name, and the fact that Godfrey doesn't have to be the winner in this situation. Maybe I'm being stupid, maybe I'm being selfish, but also it's not really me doing this. It's some other me, drunk on the crowd and trapped in the moment.

At the front, so close that I must have just missed her as I climbed onstage, is Indira. Her face is blank, her eyes are wide, as she wonders what on earth is going on. Her arms are fixed across her chest, her hair flowing down around her face and down past her shoulders, soft and shining under the assembly hall's high, bright lights. There's a twist at the side of the mouth – possibly the start of a smile – and I imagine it shifting, lifting, until a real smile is there. She'll understand what I'm doing, and who

I am, and we won't have to hide our feelings for each other any more.

'It's not Eddie,' I yell out. All the other sounds in the hall fall into silence.

'It's not Eddie,' I say again, my voice braver this time, 'it's me!'

13

'What, this guy?' someone says loudly, swiftly followed by someone else exclaiming, 'I don't even know his name!'

So I decide that perhaps the best way to say what I really want to say is to show them. I close my eyes and feel the room – so many bodies in one place. I've never tried to do anything with so many people around. What if my powers get shy? What if I start to overthink, like I did with Dr Starr, and I completely lose it? But then I feel what I'm after: that little switch of magic. My mind flies around the hall, searching for something to move that I can manage. I can feel the tension of the room, and how close it sits to my potential humiliation. I have to get this right.

There's a scrap of paper on the lectern near where Godfrey is standing. It's light enough, and simple enough for my mind to cope with. So I lift it, a simple leaf of white, lined and hole-punched, and carry it through the air so that it hovers in front of me. To be honest, it looks like a strange breeze has picked the piece of paper up and is carrying it around at random. But I know, and the other people in here know. It's me; I'm controlling it, and just like how I saw Vega work her magic on the telly, I use my arms like a concert conductor, waving and weaving so that the paper flurries and flies wherever I will it.

Eddie comes up next to me and holds out a shuttlecock that he must have found at the side of the stage. I beam at him in thanks and turn my attention away from the paper and to the light and plastic-feathered thing, swirling it up into the highest reaches of the hall, between the steel girders that support the roof, and then down towards the heads of all the gathered students. The piece of paper might not have been that impressive, but surely this will amaze the crowd!

I'm so caught up in my own perfect display that it takes me a while to tune in to the feel of everyone around me. Whereas before, it was tense with anticipation, now the atmosphere feels more subdued and stilted. I catch flickers of frowns as my focus on the shuttlecock falters, and nobody is chanting my name. Not yet.

'This is lame!' someone yells from the back.

I look around me, first at Eddie, who shrugs, and then at Godfrey, who has his arms folded across his chest and his face lined with bafflement.

'A piece of paper? A shuttlecock? Seriously?' he mutters.

But what else is there? This is all new, and I'm still learning, and who knows what might happen as my powers progress. Don't they see that? Don't they realise that this is only the start?

'So it was you? *You* broke my hand?' Godfrey holds it up at me, his hand and wrist all wrapped in solid plaster.

'You came for me. What was I supposed to do?' I say, my breathing already laboured from the effort I've put in to my little show.

'And there I was thinking that you were some sort of superpowered freak? You're nothing more than a cheap magician,' he snarls.

'I can do more,' I tell him. And then to the crowd, who are clearly wavering in their interest: 'I can do more!'

A bead of sweat on my forehead trickles down over my brow and drops to the stage as I feel out someone's rucksack on the floor below me. Somewhere behind me, Eddie, or maybe it's my conscience, is telling me to stop. It's too heavy, and I'll never manage, but I'm determined. If I'm up here, and I have to prove myself, it might as well be with something other people can really respect and admire. I'm not leaving this stage a hopeless weirdo.

The rucksack is heavy, heavier in my mind than it is in real life, and the owner steps back in disbelief as it hovers up to knee height. There it stays, despite the tension in my arms and back, despite the fact that my feet are planted apart in an action-ready power stance, and despite the brute determination I can feel all through my jaw and neck. It's so heavy, and I'm trying so hard, but all

I can manage is half a twirl before I have to let the bag go, and I lean over to cling to my knees, gasping to get my breath back.

Most of the kids here didn't even see. I didn't manage to lift it high enough. And the ones who did? They're laughing. They're all laughing at me. Maybe Dr Starr is right. I can't do anything much under pressure.

'Who does he think he is?'

'Bet you anything that the Vigils reject him.'

'I've seen way better magic tricks than that. It was all done by strings and mirrors, I bet.'

Then, as I'm still leaning over, someone farts. It's so blatantly not me who's done it, besides which the noise is obviously fake, and yet everyone is looking at me and pointing. I didn't think the laughter could get any louder. Didn't they see what I did? What about the piece of paper and the shuttlecock? If Eddie had any marbles with him I'd make them fly them too. What's wrong with these people? I reveal to the whole world that I can move things with the power of my mind, and they just don't care? I don't understand.

My eyes find Indira again. I'm hoping and praying that I see something in her eyes, something that tells me that she's impressed. But the expression on her face is confusing. She doesn't look happy. In fact, she looks the opposite of happy: she looks gutted. That's not what's meant to happen. She's meant to be impressed, and infatuated with the reveal of her mystery masked man. Instead she just looks embarrassed, even appalled.

Same goes for everybody. After the laughter dies away it's a sea of bored and disappointed faces out there. A lot of people start to leave. The worst thing is Godfrey's face. He's looking right at me, smirking. He knows that he's scored a victory; the fact that he didn't even have to get too involved to bring about my humiliation only makes it sweeter.

'So what's your superhero codename then? Fartman? With the power to trump at one hundred paces? Able to leap wet puddles and stink up tall buildings?' Godfrey laughs. Scott and the two Williams, who are standing just behind, laugh along with him.

'Leave it out, Godders,' Eddie tries, but he's not bold enough.

'Behold the mighty Fartman! Blowing people off left, right and centre!' Godfrey cackles.

I take it. I take it because I'm tired and I have no ammo left. This has been a huge disaster, and my head aches with the exertion. Why did I think I could pull off something like this? I bet it took Vega ages before she was ready to do all that stuff she did on the television. A few weeks in, and she was probably just making smoke signals. I've been an idiot, and I deserve everything Godfrey has to throw at me.

'It's OK,' Eddie says, leading me away to the backstage area. 'I mean, it was pretty much a huge disaster, but you

177

still did it! You did better than with the marbles! And before, when you said that you could only just about manage to lift a hockey stick, I mean...look what you managed today! You're already improving!'

'You don't have to be nice,' I tell him, hiding my face behind my hands. 'What have I done?'

'They'll forget about it soon enough. Just watch. I mean, I've already forgotten!'

'I'm a laughing stock.'

'No...' Eddie tries, shuffling uncomfortably on his feet. 'I mean...not really.'

'Everyone hates me.'

'Well, at least this way, now that it's all out in the open, you don't have to worry so much about it all. You can just get on with your life and be perfectly normal.'

Great, because *perfectly normal* is exactly what I wanted.

'Look, I have drama club,' Eddie says. 'Will you be OK going home on your own? Otherwise I'd invite you back to mine? Or maybe you can wait for me or something?'

'I'll be fine,' I say, even though I'm not entirely sure it's true.

On the way home I can feel my phone vibrating somewhere in my bag. I don't know who's ringing me, and I couldn't care less. It's only going to be someone making fun of me, and I can do without anyone making me feel worse than I already feel. What was I thinking? Did I really think that I was ready to demonstrate what I had? Besides which, hadn't the people at Vigil HQ warned me about this? I've really screwed it all up. What meagre chance I had of joining the Vigils has surely gone to pot now. And I didn't even check to see if anyone was filming the whole thing on their phones. I was so swept up in the possibility of glory, and of impressing Indira, that I basically lost my head. I'm an idiot. A total, waste-of-space idiot. I deserve everything that's coming to me.

I wait until I'm at home before I check my phone. Anyone looking at it would think I was the most popular boy in school. I didn't even realise that so many people had my number. Sure, there are the small smatterings of encouraging messages from people who were genuinely impressed or are being kind, but they are few and far between, and besides which, I can't tell if they're actually mocking me. The other messages are definitely from people making fun and having a go. I've been tagged in what feels like an infinite number of posts and photos on Facebook, Instagram and Twitter. Happily, you can't really tell from the photos that anything supernatural is going on, as it's just a piece of paper or a shuttlecock hanging in the air. But the video clips are slightly more incriminating. I watch just one, wincing at my own hopeful preten-tiousness. I'll have to leave the school. I'll have to leave the town. Mum and I will have to move to another planet to get away from all of this.

Just as I throw myself face down on to my bed, the phone starts vibrating again. Not the short vibrate of a message, but the long hum of a phone call. I reach over to grab it, almost forgetting that there's nobody I could possibly want to talk to right now, and answer.

'Smunfff...' I moan, holding the phone to my ear but my face still crushed into my pillow.

'Joseph? Is that you?' Great. I know the voice straight away. Just what I need. It's Agent bleeding fake-name Yellow. 'Why am I seeing what I'm seeing online?'

'Phnunfff...?'

'Joseph, this is serious. You can't go around doing this kind of thing. We warned you.'

'Fnarnfff...'

'Are you even listening to me? You've seriously jeopardised your position. What the hell were you thinking?'

I turn over on the bed and just sigh. What is there that I could possibly say? I'm going to get fired from the Vigils before I've even had a chance to join! I'm a loser – I should just give up now.

'Listen, I know you must be upset, but you have to know that you've made a lot of people here very angry and given us a lot of work to clear up.' She pauses. 'Look, we can contain the online situation, but how do we know that we can trust you? Take some time, clear your head, do whatever it is that teenage boys need to do, and someone will be in touch very soon. Oh, and Joseph?'

180

'What...?'

'If you ever cock things up like this again, you can kiss your Vigil future goodbye.'

She hangs up. I want to throw the phone across the room and pray that it gets sucked into that same mystery vortex that odd socks seem to fall into. But I don't. Because there's still one person I need to tell all this to.

Hey Mum, I text, *when are you home? We need to talk.*

'Are you all right?' she asks, handing me the mug of hot chocolate later that night. I've made her worried. She hasn't made me hot chocolate since I was twelve.

'I'm fine, Mum,' I say, but she can tell I don't mean it.

'Did something happen at that history symposium? You've not been right since then. Are you in trouble? Please, whatever it is, just tell me. I can't stand all of this mystery.'

'No, Mum, I'm not in trouble.'

'Then, Joey, what on earth is happening?'

So I tell her. I tell her everything. From the headaches and dreams, to trying to jump off the school roof, to everything that's happened this last week in London and at school. It's like I'm breathing out the whole time, letting the whole stream just pour out of me before daring to take a breath in, and I'm staring down at the coffee table, not daring to look up, too scared to see how she might be reacting.

181

'Look, I don't know about this...' Mum's fretting. 'I mean, have you tried *not* having superpowers?'

'I don't think it's a choice, Mum.'

'Are you sure? Aren't there people you can see? Aren't there scientists who know about this kind of thing?'

She's curled up around herself at the other end of the sofa and hasn't touched me since I finished telling her. I'm trying not to think about the distance between us right now, how far away she feels.

'I just want you to be happy, and to grow up and do everything that everyone else can do,' she says.

'I don't think my having powers changes that...'

'But life will be so much harder for you. The world is a dangerous place, and you can't always predict how things are going to be. I want the best for you. I want you to have the best education, and one day have a great job, so that you don't turn out like me. I want you to have *everything*, and I don't want this to get in the way of that.'

'I still think I can have everything,' I reply, even though I'm not entirely sure that I believe it. 'And think of all the opportunities for us. Think about all the places I might be able to go, and all the things I'll be able to do.' That's if I can get beyond being small fry – and don't manage to screw it all up first – but I don't voice this to Mum.

'I just want you to be normal.' Mum's eyes are heavy, with the skin underneath them smudged pink from tears. She can barely look at me.

'I am normal. I'm exactly the same person I was before . . . with just a bit extra, that's all. It's just a talent, like if I was really good at piano or something.'

'Look, I still love you – please don't ever doubt that – but this might take a little while to sink in, OK? I just need to adjust.'

'I thought you'd be happy for me,' I admit. 'I thought you'd be excited.'

'I just don't want everything we've been working towards to go to waste. I don't want you to throw it all away because of some dream.'

'Mum, this isn't a dream. Look . . .'

I glance back down at the coffee table, crowded with old magazines she brings home from the client reception area at work, some cotton pads that Mum's used the other night to wipe off her nail polish and a couple of my textbooks. First I try to lift up the remote control, but it's too heavy and I'm too emotional to focus. So I go for the used cotton pads instead and I bring them over to my hand, in as smooth and controlled a motion as I can manage, which isn't much to be honest.

'You really did that? With no strings or secret magic tricks?'

'See this too . . .' Without even looking over at the light switch – just seeing it psychically in my head – I flick the ceiling light off. And on again, and off again.

'OK, OK, stop that,' Mum says.

'This is who I am now,' I sigh.

'You just need to give me time to get used to it all. It's not every day you come home from work to discover that your son has been abducted by Vigil agents and taken to London. Everything I thought I knew about you, it's all just been flipped over in one evening.'

'I don't think I was abducted . . . not exactly . . .'

'So what happens next?'

'I'm not sure . . . I think I've ruined everything before it's even begun.'

'You're not going to disappear off to London anytime soon?'

'Not unless you want me to . . .?'

Finally Mum breaks out of her bubble of confusion and shuffles over to me. She looks at me long and hard in the eyes, as if trying to work out whether I'm still the same person, before wrapping me up in one of her biggest, tightest hugs.

'No matter what you decide to do,' she says, 'you'll always be my little boy. A part of me wishes that you never have to grow up and can stay with me for ever.'

We stay hugging, tightly wound up in each other, for a long time, before a yawn on my part breaks the spell.

'You must be exhausted,' Mum says.

'It's been a long day.' I yawn again. 'A really weird and horrible long day.'

I go to bed, and just as I lay my head back down on the

184

pillow I hear it, a soft sound from the room next door, muffled but definitely audible through our paper-thin walls. Mum is crying. When I close my eyes I wonder whether if I really tried hard enough I could see through the walls, just to check in and see that she's OK, but then what would be the point? Because I know that she's not, and I don't think that watching her cry would do me any good. I tell myself that it'll be all right in the end, that Mum will come around, and get used to this strange new thing, but there's a secret fear as well. There's a fear that somehow I've driven an impossible wedge between us, and that things will never be like they were. It makes me want to cry too.

14

Life is singularly crap. Waking up is crap, getting out of bed is crap, and putting on my school uniform – all complete and utter crap. I might have won the lottery, but my prize is only a tenner. What are you meant to do with a tenner? Nothing good can be bought for that much. Nothing even worth telling people about. And yet here I am, having told and shown people everyone what I can do, and it's all worse than if I'd done nothing at all.

Mum doesn't knock on my door after her shower to check if I'm up. I can hear her getting busy, hear the hairdryer blasting, and I know that she's not smiling. That she wishes she could stay home today, crying into endless cups of tea. I thought I was giving her everything. I thought that maybe, perhaps, our life could change, but if anything I've made things worse. Is she scared of me now? Scared of what I've become, and what I might be able to do? I haven't got the heart to tell her that I'm barely more impressive than a stupid magician at a children's birthday party. That people are laughing at me. That I hate myself.

This was not the way it was meant to be.

I'm not going to school. I don't think Mum expects me to go either. I hear her leave the house for work, and she doesn't say anything. I might be risking a black mark against my scholarship, but if ever there was a need for a personal day, I think this would be it. I already have my trousers, socks and my shirt on, but I haven't the heart to fix my tie.

Not coming in today, I message Eddie.

To his credit, he replies pretty much straight away: *Don't worry, I'll get the homework for you.*

I flop back on my bed, still half dressed, moan and crush my face back into the pillow.

If there is one thing I am not expecting in a million years, it's a message from Indira.

I haven't been able to escape the image of her face in the assembly hall. She looked like she was dying of embarrassment. She had made no secret of how she felt for the mystery masked man, and now she has to deal with the fact that her hero was – is – me. Must be such a letdown.

I'm sorry that I allowed her to be humiliated. I'm sorry that I made her think that I was someone I wasn't, and didn't tell her the truth before she put her own heart on the line.

Can you meet me in Gatford shopping centre after school? I'll be at the coffee place in the court.

187

Huh?

I can't even articulate properly what my brain is going through. There are lots of questions spinning around in my head. Does she just want to shout at me? Maybe it would be better if I just stayed away...

I decide to go, because of course I can't stay away from her. She's *Indira*. But I've also decided not to get my hopes up. I'll just let her talk, let her vent her feelings, and then take myself home. It's the least I can do, and maybe it would make going back into school again on Monday a little easier.

Getting off the bus at the shopping centre, I linger outside the automatic doors for longer than necessary, checking my phone for the millionth time, just to make sure that I haven't dreamt up this rendezvous. I see on all the sites that the pictures of me are still being shared, but now everyone is saying things like, 'This is a fake. No Vigil in Gatford' and, 'Guys, whatever you say, if the Vigils haven't confirmed it, then it's probably not real. Looks rubbish anyway!' I briefly wonder why the Vigils wouldn't put out a denial, but I guess that giving no comment is the best strategy to take the heat out of the situation and make people lose interest. I quickly check one last time that it's definitely Indira that messaged me – it's from the same account that messaged me about the history homework, so this is probably not going to be a wind-up. I remind myself that she's set the meeting, that she is the one who has something to say to me, and that I can walk away at any time if I want to. If I can.

At first when I get to the cafe in the central court I don't see Indira. My eyes are peeled for her hair, her face, but there's nothing. Maybe this has been a wind-up after all . . . but then, as I get closer, I realise that she's hunched over a table wearing an oversized Gatford House hockey hoodie, with the hood pulled right up over her head. So she's embarrassed then, and doesn't want to be seen with me. At least that's a scenario I'm mentally prepared for.

She looks over both shoulders as I sit down, checking to see if there's anyone around who would notice us being together.

'Do you want a drink?' I ask, because I feel it's the polite thing to do, not because I want to endear myself to her.

'I'm fine,' she replies, hands gripped tight around a mug of something that looks like it might have a complicated name.

To be honest I'm relieved – I can't afford the drinks in this place anyway.

'Um . . . Are you OK?'

I try to start the conversation off, because she can't even seem to be able to look me in the eye. I can see her though. As I settle into my seat I can see her face, which for once is completely make-up free. I don't comment about how she looks. Because I know that I'm probably the one who made her like this.

189

'It was really you? The other day? In the mask?' she asks, a sad wobble in her voice.

I nod in reply and let my head drop. I stare at her coffee cup, and then have to look sharply away when I realise that my gaze and focus is making it shift. Only imperceptibly, but I don't want to risk causing an accident and spilling it everywhere.

'You should have told me. When we were in the library. You should have said something when I was making a total idiot of myself.'

I'm relieved that she doesn't seem more angry, but then I don't know how to respond when she's being all sad like this. I hang my head lower, and wait for the insults.

'You know that I ruined what I had with Godfrey for you?' She waits expectantly, so I think I'm meant to say something.

'He's a prat,' I say finally, surprised at my own candour. 'You really can't see that?'

'Yeah, well. There I was thinking my mystery saviour was going to be different. But after what happened in assembly yesterday... Do you even realise how stupid you looked? Was it worth it?'

I shrug and have to sit on my hands to stop myself fidgeting. 'I'm sorry.' It hangs there, sounding pathetic.

'It was so embarrassing, Wilco. I can't believe what I said... that you didn't stop me!'

'I'm really sorry,' I say. 'I was told I had to keep quiet

about my real identity. I couldn't even tell you...' I really don't have anything else to offer. 'I wish I knew a way to make it all right, but I don't.'

'Well...there is one way you can make it up to me,' she says suddenly. The tone has changed. She sounds softer, less cruel and accusing. 'You *can* make it up to me, if you want to.'

I look up for the first time in what feels like ages.

'I know you're not like all those rugby guys I usually hang out with. I know that you're better than they are.'

'I'm not better than anyone...' I mope.

'But you like me, right?'

What am I meant to do? I'm too shy to say yes or even nod my head, but I do manage to bring my eyes up and meet hers. That's all she needs.

'You like me. And I'm a fair person. So I'm going to give you the chance to make it up to me.'

'How?'

'Godfrey has something of mine. A phone. One of those cheap ones. I got it for him so that we could be private. We could say private things and stuff, and our parents wouldn't know. It was meant to be romantic. Anyway. It's got personal things on it. Things I don't want anyone to see. And Godfrey won't give it back.'

'A phone?'

'Loads of people do it. Tasha Fitzpatrick has three: one for school, one for family and one for dating. It works.

So, look, there's stuff on that phone, really private stuff, and Godfrey's basically holding it to ransom from me. I'm scared that if this goes on much longer, he'll make what's on the phone public. And that can't happen. Trust me.'

My mind is ablaze with awkward thoughts of what could possibly be on that phone. Could they be . . . OK, I'm not going to go there. Too much for me to cope with.

She rolls her eyes, frustrated at herself, and then takes a long sip of her drink.

'You want me to get it back for you? How?'

'His family are going out on Saturday night. Some big celebration. And anyway, Godfrey's been gloating to everyone about how they're all going to this Michelin-starred restaurant. They'll be out, and the house will be empty. I know the security code because I've seen him enter it loads of times and I know where he's stashed the phone. It'll be easy. You go in there, get it back and this will all be over.'

'You want me to break into the Chappells' house? That's against the law, Indira.'

'Look, what's more wrong? You going in there to get something that rightfully belongs to me, or him basically blackmailing me? You'll be preventing something much bigger happening. It's for the greater good. I'll never make head girl if the stuff on that phone gets out. And you have these powers now. They must come in useful for something, right? Think of this as your first Vigil mission.'

'What does he want you to do to give it back?' I'm not sure that I want to hear the answer.

'You know what boys are like . . .'

No. I don't know. Not boys like them. And I don't want to. I shuffle uncomfortably.

'I suppose you think I'm going to just comply – *Wilco* and all that?'

'Joseph . . .' She uses my real name. I didn't even know if she knew it. 'Joseph, if you did this for me, then I would never forget it. It would mean so much to me, and I think that it would mean that we could really be friends. I'd like that. Wouldn't you?'

I would. I can't deny it. In fact, I'd like to be more than friends, but I'm not sure how I'm meant to tell her. Maybe this can be the start though? Maybe, if I help her with this one thing, everything else will be easier?

'I know it's short notice, but I think tomorrow night might be the only chance. There's always so much security around the house when they're in – his dad is a politician, did you know that? – but when they're all out together, the security guys go with them. Plus, I know where he's keeping the phone.'

'So why can't *you* go in and get it? If this plan is so foolproof, why don't you just rock up and take it back?' I'm surprised at the force in my voice, especially after being quiet for so long.

'Joseph,' she says my name again, her voice so sweet

and warm, 'I'm already busy on Saturday night. I can't just blow my friends off like that. They can't know about this whole mess – it's so embarrassing, and plus, you know, you have powers now?'

'I thought we had already established that my powers aren't "worth it".'

'I know, but it must make some things easier. Like being sneaky, or something.'

'Why would I have to be sneaky? If you know all the codes and everything.'

'Listen, you do me this one favour, and we'll forget about everything. We'll forget about how you scared the bejesus out of me last week in that mask, and we'll forget about you letting me make a total fool out of myself in the library the other day. What you did wasn't all that nice, you know? You're lucky I'm even sitting here with you.'

'Look, Indira, I'm sorry about all of that—'

'All you have to do is this one tiny favour – and you'd be really saving my skin. My parents would disown me if some of those things got out. My life would be over! Just this one favour, and then we can forget about this whole ugly mess. I'll pretend that it never happened.'

'Really?' I do feel awful about how it all went. I'd love for her to just blank it all out of her mind.

'Of course! I'd be in *your* debt. And, I suppose, we could get to know each other a little better?'

194

She really is a damsel in distress. I could save her. I know that she's probably promising more than she really means to give, but if I play the gallant knight this one time, then she'll see me. Really *see* me. I won't be Wilco any more after this. I'll be something more, at least to her. The instinct is there, burning inside me: to prove to her that I am worthy.

After the misery of yesterday, and the depressive gloom of today, is it really so bad that I want to do something bold and good? My powers will get stronger, and I'll get bolder, and one day soon I won't be a laughing stock any more.

'You're certain that they're all going to be out?' I ask.

'Absolutely. Godfrey's great-grandmother has just turned one hundred or something, and they're going out to celebrate. They'll be out for hours. They have a driver who takes them places, and the Chappells like to drink. You'll have hours and hours to get it done. You go in, go to Godfrey's room, get the phone and leave. I can meet you on Sunday to pick it up. Godfrey won't even know anything is wrong. Until he sees the phone has gone of course. Can you imagine his face? I honestly can't believe that we were ever an item. It all seems so silly now, don't you think?'

'And there's no way you can be there? Waiting outside or something, just to make sure that everything goes down OK?'

'I told you, I have a party to go to. I can't let my friends down. They'll be expecting me, and they'll know something's wrong if I don't turn up. You'll be fine. I'll have my other phone with me all night so you can call me if you have any problems. Shall I give you my number?'

She says that last sentence slowly, knowingly.

'OK...' I reply, my voice cracking slightly, but I think I cover it well.

Indira takes my phone and puts in her details. Indira's number, in my phone. I can text her now. Not stupid little messages over websites. Having someone's phone number means something. It means something important.

'There.' She calls her own number from my phone so that my details flash up on her screen. 'And now I have yours. I'll text you the security code.'

'What kind of problems do you think there'd be?'

'What?'

'Problems. You said to call you if there were any problems. What problems?'

'Oh, that's just a saying, silly. Nothing will go wrong. Bish, bash, bosh. Done.' She brings a hand up to my face and touches my cheek. 'You really are very sweet, you know?'

I'd love to say that I had something cool and macho to say in response to this, but stuck in the moment, all I can do is endure the awkward blush.

'You really are sweet,' she reiterates. 'And when this whole mess is over, I won't forget it. This means so much to me, and you'll be my hero.'

As if I hadn't already decided to help her, those last few words seal my fate. Being a hero means everything. And if it can only ever be for Indira, then so be it. Being one person's hero is better than being no hero at all.

15

Godfrey's house is amazing.

It's not just big, or grand, or comfortable; it's all of those things a million times over. He actually doesn't live all that far away from Eddie, but while the Olsens' place is big in a relatively normal way, this house is big in a way that screams wealth and power.

All the houses on this street have driveways and large front gardens. They're all detached, and all different – some mock Tudor, some more Victorian-looking and some that are modern and, frankly, a little bizarre. I can immediately tell which house belongs to the Chappells because it's the only one that has been fenced off and gated. You can barely see it from the road, as behind the tall gates are some oversized, proud conifers. To be honest, if you didn't know that there was a house hiding behind there, you might be tempted just to walk on and ignore it, which I suppose is the point.

There's a gap in the fence. I only know it's there because Indira told me about it. Godfrey uses it to sneak in and out of the house without his parents knowing. She told me that he likes to smoke, and if anyone ever found out what it is that he likes to smoke, then he'd be in big trouble. She wouldn't look me in the eye when we talked about the smoking, which made me think that she's not exactly the perfect prefect-wannabe I always presumed she was.

The gap was exactly where Indira said it would be. You have to go down the drive of the house next door to find it, but it's there. One of the iron railings is loose, and I can just about crawl through before battling the conifers to get to the driveway. There's already a gap and the barest hint of a path, which suggests to me that this route is one that's used often.

The next challenge is getting to the spare key. Apparently the Chappells have this hi-tech key keeper that needs a code. But it's OK, because Indira has given me this too. The key keeper is secreted away behind a nook in the entryway, and when I enter the correct code it flips open, revealing the treasure within.

I take a moment to consider how well this is all going, and then my phone vibrates. It's Indira, asking if everything is OK. I like knowing that she's thinking of me right now. It's reassuring. I text her back, saying everything is fine and I'm about to go in.

The key fits in the front door, which is about double the width of mine at home. It turns smoothly, and the door opens. There's a couple of seconds of blissful silence for me to consider the grandness of the Chappells' entryway before I hear the dark drone of the alarm system. It's making a very urgent noise, demanding to be switched off. But I don't worry, because Indira has told me where to find the panel and what the code is. Apparently Godfrey isn't as security conscious as the rest of his family.

I press on the numbers, my phone out so I can look at the screen and check that they're the right ones as I'm keying them in.

Four-five-four-six-eight-two, and then the letter *A*.

Who knows what mystical meaning that series of numbers has, but I key it in, expecting the horrible droning to stop the moment I finish the sequence. So far Indira's intel has been flawless after all.

It doesn't. The noise doesn't stop. I look down at my phone again, recheck the numbers and go over them in my head – quickly because my heart is already racing – and type them in one more time. I wait a second for the alarm to stop – I give it a chance – before I realise that something is very wrong. The code Indira gave me doesn't work.

Could the alarm code have changed? I type furiously to her. No reply.

The droning beeps get louder. I can't have long before the main alarm is triggered. How long do these things usually take? Do they give you thirty seconds? A minute?

I stare at my phone, the screen empty, praying for Indira to reply with a correction, but she doesn't. It's only now that it hits me: I've broken into a house. Not just any house, but a politician's house. It doesn't matter how heroic I thought I was being, this is definitely wrong and I really shouldn't be here.

I start to flail – really flail. I turn in circles on the spot, looking around me for any clue that might get me out of this mess. I suppose the only thing is to go back out the way I came and make a run for it. But is it too late? Am I on camera? Have I tripped some invisible wire, causing the police to jump out of their seats and into their cars? Should I run upstairs and grab the phone now? If the full alarm siren starts, that's only going to mean trouble for me.

My panic blooms into something that hurts, something that makes me want to be sick, and then the wailing starts.

As if in response to my crazed panic, I start to feel shapes and textures in my mind. The eyes in my mind reach out, and with invisible fingers I can feel the marbled floor, cool and solid beneath me. Nearby there's an ornament on a small table, and it begins to shudder as my awareness of it grows. It doesn't even take that much energy or focus, just the force of my fear and the adrenaline sweeping through me seems to be enough to move, well, everything. The curtains at the window, the paintings on the wall and the little ornaments that seem to be everywhere – I can feel them all in my mind as they start to move. Only small vibrations, nothing extreme, but the sudden influx of objects and textures in my head makes me want to cave in on myself. It's too much information at once, and all set to the piercing background noise of the siren. I'm standing in a mini-earthquake of my own making, paralysed by my fear and the vast array of neurons sparking fireworks in my head.

When the noise suddenly deadens into nothing, the only sound left is my own screaming. I'm on the floor, arms wrapped around my knees, holding myself together as tightly as possible as though my limbs might all come away from my body and scatter with my own power. My scream continues, eerily matching the tone of the now silenced alarm. Eventually, slowly, like waking from a nightmare, I bring my head up and let myself adjust to the sudden silence.

The noise echoes through my head for a while longer, ringing in my ears, but otherwise everything is calm. The shuddering has stopped, the noise has stopped, and things are all as they should be.

Except... I turn around to look at the alarm keypad by the door. Which is now closed. There's a girl standing there. She looks kind of like Kesia. She's holding a device up to the alarm panel and fixing it there.

'It's OK,' the Kesia lookalike says. 'I've deactivated it.'

Kesia? Is it her? She never mentioned that she had an

older sister, and yet that's the only way I seem to be able to comprehend what I'm looking at. It's Kesia, but she's also different. Older, assertive, and really, shockingly...hot.

'You –' she turns to look right at me, her eyes burning like lasers – 'are the biggest idiot I have ever come across. What the hell are you doing here?'

My mouth opens, but no sound comes out. I don't even think I manage to blink.

She's wearing skin-tight black: black combat trousers and a black vest under a black jacket, half zipped up. She's also wearing some kind of belt with pockets, and black biker boots. Her reddish-brown hair is tied back in a sharp ponytail; I'm used to seeing it down and around her face. Now that it's pulled back, I can see the angles of her face more clearly. Who even knew that she had cheekbones?

I try and say her name. I try and say anything.

'Get up off the floor!' she shouts at me. 'We've got work to do before we get out of here.'

What? I only just discover that she can talk, and she's already yelling at me?

'Kes...' The sound comes out, and I know that I want to say her name, but I'm also slightly scared of it.

'I said, get up!' she yells again, this time marching over and heaving me up by the shoulder.

The moment I'm on my feet I shudder out of her grasp and back away from her, feeling my way until I'm sitting

203

down again on some sort of antique bench. Right now, for some reason, I definitely feel as if I need to be sitting. There's still the ringing in my head for starters, and the fact that Kesia's gaze is so focused and accusing. What the hell is all of this?

Perhaps she realises how scared I am, or how confused, I don't know, but all at once her shoulders seem to relax and her face softens.

She lets out a tired sigh before explaining all at once: 'I'm not who you think I am. I'm not a student at Gatford House. I'm not even fifteen. I'm eighteen, and I work for the Vigils. They call me Kittyhawk. I've been undercover. Initially it was to keep tabs on Godfrey Chappell, to try to find a way to get close to his father, but once we found out about you, well, my position was convenient. I've been trailing you, and trying to make sure that you stay out of trouble. Guess I haven't done a very good job. Now, will you tell me what the hell you think you're doing in Douglas Chappell's house?'

I suppose she thought it would be like ripping off a plaster: one sharp tug of pain, followed by the sting of awareness. The point being that it would hurt less in the long run. But yet, here I am, the plaster off, and the stinging goes on. I stare at her, barely blinking, my jaw still hanging loose.

She sighs again and looks up to the ceiling, obviously frustrated with me and my inability to be cool.

'Look, this is how we do things. Covert, undercover, so that no one knows. It makes sense when you do what we do. And it works. In the end it works, and people don't get hurt. I'm sorry that I had to lie to you, and to Eddie. I am, but this is my job. Do you follow?'

I think I'm nodding. I'm not sure because my head still feels so light and strange, but I try to show that I understand at least. I still can't move though. It isn't just the shock of seeing Kesia here, but it's all those other feelings too: the earthquake that I managed to cause, and all that noise.

'I promise we can talk about this some more,' Kesia says, her voice softer. 'I know that this is hard for you. But right now, I need you to be cool. I need you to stand up, and stay with me. Don't go out of my sight. I have a job to do, and after that I have to get us both out of here. Can you do that? Will you be OK?'

I nod again, properly this time. I can do this. If I want to be one of them, I have to prove that I can handle this kind of drama.

She rests a hand on my shoulder again – I think she's trying to be comforting but it seems awkward for her – and I stand, trying to look brave.

'Does Eddie know?' I manage to ask her.

'No,' Kesia says shortly. 'Are you going to explain why *you* are here?'

'Are you going to tell him?'

'No. And you can't either.' She's looking around for something.

'But...' I want to tell her that he's in love with her, but I'm not entirely sure how appropriate that would be.

'We'll talk about Eddie later, OK? Right now I need you to do as I say. I don't know why you're here, but seeing as you've led me into this mess, we might as well make some use of it. Douglas Chappell has an offline private computer, and I need the intel from it. Stay close to me, OK? We haven't got long before they discover that the alarm has been hot-wired. Once I've got the information I need, we're going to need to get out of here fast. Do you think you'll be OK?'

'Yes.' I say it out loud, because I want her to know she can be sure of me.

'Good, then let's go.'

I follow Kesia – Agent Kittyhawk – through the house, scanning around using the eyes in my mind to see further through any open doors. There are formal front rooms and less formal back rooms, all highly stylised and comfortable looking. It's like walking through a show home. The place is also so immaculate that I can't imagine anyone actually living here. Eddie's place was always clean and tidy, but there was a certain busy-ness to it, that made the rooms feel welcoming and homely. This house looks so polished and new I'm not sure anyone has ever actually sat at that dining-room table or lounged on that sofa. Have any of those sparkling kitchen appliances ever been used? The only hint that this really is a family home is all the photographs. They're everywhere. On the walls, on shelves and countertops, and all framed in gold or silver. There's Godfrey's father, smiling his big, toothy politician's smile, his eyes crinkling with the effort. There's his wife (whose name I don't know) who has hair bleached so blonde that it looks nearly white, and gleaming white teeth to match. Godfrey looks so much like a younger version of his father that I find it quite uncanny, and then there's the younger sister (who doesn't go to Gatford so I've never met her), so sweet that looking at her makes my teeth hurt. None of them look real. It's like they're an alien family who are so desperate to prove that they're definitely a happy human one that they've gone too far the other way. It unsettles me. It makes me want to call home and tell my mum how much I love her.

We arrive in an office, decorated to look like it's an old-fashioned stately study. The walls are wood-panelled and book-lined, and the desk is absolutely huge. Behind the desk is a massive old-fashioned high-backed chair with dimples in its rich-red leather.

'He keeps his computer in his desk drawer, but it's locked. You didn't see me do this, OK? Just turn round, and keep an eye on the door.'

She doesn't seem to realise that just because I'm not looking at something doesn't mean that I can't see it. Kesia reaches into a zip pouch on her belt, pulls out a clip, and starts working at the lock on Mr Chappell's desk.

'OK,' she says, when the drawer clicks open, 'now to business.'

'You know what you're doing?' I ask Kesia, and then instantly hate myself because of course she knows what she's doing, why wouldn't she? She works for the Vigils.

Kesia sits in the chair and reaches into another pocket to find a flash drive. She inserts it into the computer, which is now sitting up on the desk. 'Booting it up now... Oh, look, his password is exactly the one he uses for his work computer. OK... This little baby should do all the work for me.'

'What are you looking for exactly?' I ask, even though I'm not sure I even want to know.

'You know about the Ditko Finance building fire?' she checks, swivelling in the chair and eyeing me closely.

'Of course... Do you really think that Godfrey's dad had something to do with that?'

'Well, it's been suspected for some time that the *Honourable* Douglas Chappell has more to do with that than he claims. Instead of doing his job, which is to ensure that bribes and scams *don't* happen, he's been running a tidy little business making sure that his best friends are well protected. Plus he has a dark past with Ditko. So of course both he and Ditko Finance wanted their building to burn. Decades' worth of evidence was lost, just when the company was due to be investigated for major fraud. It would have exposed all his dealings with them too. We think Chappell's job was to ensure the Vigils didn't get there in time to stop the plan from going ahead. The only problem? The place was meant to be empty. Nobody was meant to die.'

I think fast. 'But the Vigils aren't corrupt though, are they? I mean, they can do what they want, right? They don't have to do anything if they think it's for a bad person or bad reasons?'

'Look, the big catastrophic fires and floods and the odd tornado are always going to get looked after. The Government doesn't have anything to do with the stuff that gets the big coverage. But there are countless smaller operations that you never hear about going on all the time. Trust me – the Vigils don't just sit around waiting for danger to hit. We're always busy, always got plenty going on. Now supposedly we're always doing what's good for society and making sure that the world is a safer place. But people like Douglas Chappell try to ruin it and turn it all into a game of strategy and profit. He thought that delaying the saving or salvaging of an office building would slip under the radar. But people dying and being injured needlessly tends to have the opposite effect.'

'So why don't you stop him?' As I say it, there's a ping from the computer and Kesia swivels back around to remove the flash drive.

'Because we need proof.' She grins, holding it up. 'I'll be honest with you, Wilco, this evening was meant to just be me keeping an eye on you and making sure that you didn't get into trouble. But, as you can't stay out of trouble for more than two seconds, I thought that we'd use the opportunity of being in here to get some real work done. My bosses have been wanting to get something on Chappell for ages, but breaking into his house was always a no-go. Too much risk, not enough preliminary evidence, yadda yadda yadda. There's always some excuse. But the order to trail you conveniently overrides the old order, so here we are, and man, are the guys at the Strand going to be thrilled when I call this in!' She switches off the laptop and replaces it in the desk exactly how it was.

'And what happens after? When you expose Douglas Chappell for who he really is?'

'He resigns from office, gets prosecuted and goes to prison for a while,' Kesia replies.

'Godfrey's dad is going to go to prison?'

'Please don't be thinking about poor little Godfrey after everything that's happened. We both know he's a nightmare. Well, turns out apples don't fall far from the tree. Douglas Chappell is a bad man who found his way to a position of power. He's made it hard for us to bring him down, but now we should have what we need. And the best thing as far as you're concerned is that I'll tell my bosses at HQ that you helped. I'll tell them that you're onside, and that you're someone we can trust. It'll stand you in good stead once you're older and out of school, especially after that god-awful stunt you pulled the other day. Do you even realise how much trouble you've caused? Now, we should really be getting out of here!'

I follow Kesia back the way we came, until we're in the smart entrance hall. She goes back over to the device she left on the alarm keypad, removes it, and starts pressing buttons.

'Wait!' I call out to her.

'What?'

'The phone! That's the whole reason I'm here! I need to get Indira's phone back.'

'All this effort for a phone?'

'Godfrey's blackmailing Indira with some of the stuff he's got on there. Indira sent me to get it back for her.'

'Well, aren't you a knight in shining armour? Look, kid, leave it. Girls are going to take stupid photos and send them to stupid boys for the rest of time. We're going to be out of here in seconds and we can put this whole operation behind us. It's just a stupid phone.'

'I said I'd do it for Indira,' I insist, but as I turn to the staircase I see Kesia roll her eyes.

'Wilco!' she calls after me.

'My name is Joseph!' I yell back from halfway up the stairs.

Her intel on the security code might have been dodgy,

211

but everything else Indira told me has been sound. Godfrey's room is exactly where she told me it would be (and I can tell that it's definitely his because of the school books and rugby kit lying around), and I spot the desk drawers where the phone is being kept almost straight away. I try not to dwell on the fact that I'm in the bedroom of my mortal enemy, but focus on the mission, and imagine how happy and relieved Indira is going to be that I've got this back for her.

'She's not worth it, you know,' Kesia says, standing in the doorway and leaning on one hip. 'You think that this will win her over, but it won't. She's using you.'

'You did your job,' I reply, 'and now I have to do mine. I'm not leaving here without the phone.'

'Whatever. Just hurry up, OK?' She paces over to the window and checks outside.

In the top desk drawer is a box, and in the box is the phone. I wonder if I should look at the photos. It's not as if anyone would know if I did, but no; Indira implied that the shots were personal, presumably risqué, and I don't think that I'd want to see anything that would degrade her in any way. I'm still looking at the phone when I hear it.

There's a noise downstairs, and like startled meerkats both Kesia and I straighten up and look to the door.

'Darling? Did you not set the alarm before we went out?' we hear a man's voice downstairs say.

It's the Chappells. They're home.

16

We're both hiding in Godfrey's walk-in wardrobe, and I'm far closer to Kesia than I think Eddie would like. I mean, it's not as if I can help it, and I can barely even see her for goodness sake, but still, I'm uncomfortable in more ways than one.

The door to the closet is closed, but the light from Godfrey's room comes in through the slats, painting lines on Kesia's face. Her brow is furrowed – she's annoyed.

'I knew we should have gone when I said,' she hisses at me.

'I had to get the phone,' I hiss back. 'That was the whole point of being here.'

'Shhh.' She gives me an angry thump on the arm. I want to tell her that she was the one who started talking to me, not the other way around, but I'm also pretty scared of her right now. 'Keep quiet. We'll find a way out of here.'

'Can't you call for backup or anything?'

213

'And admit that we've broken in here? I'm not even meant to be in here. My task was to trail you, and make sure that you didn't get up to any funny business.'

'So what about getting the drive from Godfrey's dad's computer?'

'That was my own initiative. But if the Strand finds out what I did, without authorisation or backup, I could been in trouble too. We need to get out of here before anyone realises what's going on. If Douglas Chappell even suspects that he's being investigated, it could all be over.'

She gives me another thump to warn me to stay quiet, when we hear footsteps coming up the stairs. Having her thump my arm isn't exactly helping me stay calm. I mean, what the hell? If Godfrey finds me in here, my life will be over. Never mind Kesia's secret mission and how important that might be, we're talking about my life here. Godfrey would legitimately kill me.

As my heart rate quickens I bunch my hands up around some old things that are lying on the floor around me. I can't tell if they're clean clothes or dirty laundry, and I don't care. I could be holding on to Godfrey's stinking underpants right now and it wouldn't bother me – I just need to grip on to something, anything, to keep myself calm.

'You OK?' Kesia asks. She must have realised just how scared I am. 'Just focus on deep breathing. And don't get all freaky-telekinetic on me, all right? We'll make it out of here.'

I think it might be too late not to get *all freaky-telekinetic*. Already my senses are hyperaware, and I feel everything with a heightened sensitivity. When I close my eyes the tiny, dark world around me is vividly clear. I can see it all, and all it would take to move anything would be a mental nudge, a gentle push. Am I stronger now? Or is it all down to the adrenaline and fear? Because everything around me feels lighter, as if it wouldn't be nearly so tough to make more things happen.

'Slow breathing,' Kesia whispers to me. 'Nice and calm. When they're all downstairs, watching TV, we'll creep out the back, OK? But you have to keep calm. It'll all be over soon.'

Godfrey comes into his bedroom. He sits down at his desk, turns on his computer and some music and starts singing. I've never heard him sing before, and it turns out there's a reason for that. He sounds terrible. He is completely and ridiculously tone deaf. I won't lie – there's a part of me that's desperate to record this on my phone and play it in school on Monday – but I'm just too scared. So instead I give Kesia a look (she gives me a look right back) and we hunker down, listening to him wailing something about never forgetting the good times, and silently urging him to go downstairs.

It occurs to me that he might not go back downstairs, that Godfrey might not leave his room again until the morning. This isn't going to work. Just hiding and waiting is not going to work. The clothes hanging up around us waver as if in a breeze.

'Joseph,' Kesia warns under her breath, 'keep it cool.'

I'm trying, I really am. I'm not letting my mind focus on anything in particular – but I seem to be drawn to a trainer on the floor in front of me, and my mind starts fixating on it and it starts to rattle with tension. I move on to something else. Letting my mind sit for too long on one thing seems to mean that I start to feel it in my head, and then, as I panic, I can't seem to get it out of my head. As instinctual as a sneeze or a yawn, the need to feel and move the things around me is difficult to resist.

Godfrey turns his music up really loud. There are thumping guitars and the heavy bass booms through my chest while he yells out the lyrics at the top of his voice. Kesia, silent next to me, buries her face in her knees, obviously exasperated and tired, while I try and peer through the slats of the wardrobe door, seeing even further around the corners of the room with the psychic eyes in my mind. I'm watching and waiting for my enemy to go away. Would you believe it, he's dancing. Actually dancing. Well, as much as you can dance with your left hand in a plaster cast. He's yelling tunelessly and throwing his head around, rocking to his own private rave and getting the words wrong.

'Godfrey!' someone calls from downstairs. Must be his father. 'Turn that god-awful wretched music down!'

'Can't hear you!' Godfrey calls back, before slamming his bedroom door closed and turning the music up even louder.

'We need to get out of here,' I mutter to Kesia, feeling bold enough to talk because of the volume of the music.

'You just need to hold on and be quiet,' Kesia whispers back to me. I think I liked her better when she hardly said a word. And then: 'Isn't there something you can do? With your powers? Like a distraction or something?'

I think. And then I decide to open his bedroom door. *If I could just get him out of the room . . .* I work the door handle with barely any effort, and then tug the door ajar. Godfrey doesn't notice it at first, but the almighty noise that he's playing must be carrying, because there's his dad yelling at him again to turn it down. But before Godfrey even has a chance to get up and close the door my mind is already out in the hallway, seeing and feeling and flying and hungering for something to grab on to. As soon as I find the vase, made of etched glass and filled with flowers, I push at it, so that it tumbles off its little table and falls to the floor with a smash and clatter.

Godfrey immediately sits up straight.

'GODFREY!' There's his dad again, sounding fierce and lion-like.

Godfrey runs out of the room to see what's happened. Kesia looks sharply at me, and tugs at my arm so harshly that I nearly drop the phone.

'Come on!' she orders as I shove it in my pocket.

Kesia taking the lead, we quietly push open the wardrobe door and stalk through his room. I was thinking that we could make a dash for it through the open door and hide somewhere else in the house. But she's dragging me over to his window.

'What are you doing? We can't go out the window!' I whisper-shout against the music.

'Well, we're not going out the front door,' Kesia replies, levering the window open. 'Come on, this opens out on to a back extension. It's not a big drop, but we have to move NOW.'

Standing up on the windowsill, she slinks herself legs-first through the window, in a motion so fluid I suspect that she's done it before, and drops out on to the flat roof of the extension below. She barely makes any noise at all save for a soft whoosh, and has somehow managed to make her escape look simple and elegant. I peer down at her; it's not far. I can do this. It'll be a tight squeeze through the window, and Godfrey will know something's not right the moment he comes back into the room and finds it ajar, but I have to try.

'What the?!'

I'm sitting on the window sill, my legs dangling outside, when Godfrey comes back in.

'Come on!' Kesia calls from below, but I don't know if I can do it, not now, and not with Godfrey right behind me.

'Wilco? What the hell are you doing? Hey!' he yells over the top of his stupidly loud music, with more confusion than rage in his voice. And then, with a sudden blaze of realisation, 'Dad! DAD!'

I don't so much jump as let myself fall, the flat roof below coming up sooner than I expected. Kesia grabs my arm and pulls me over to the side, pushing my body flush up against the side of the house.

'What now? What now?' I ask, panicked and scared.

'Just stay with me. We can still get out of this, but I need you to stay calm.'

'I take it back, I don't want to be a hero. Not like this!'

'Shut up,' says Kesia. 'Just shut up and stick close.'

She doesn't let go of my sleeve as she pulls me around to the side of the house. Just as we're about to disappear around the corner, Godfrey pokes his head out of his bedroom window.

'Don't go anywhere! We've got you! We've got you, Wilco!' he calls out. He almost sounds excited, jubilant, as if this might be the best fun he's had in ages.

For me, not so much. Kesia's already roaming spider-like over the sloping tiles that make up this part of the roof. She doesn't look down, only forward, and I honestly don't know how she's managing not to fall off. I pray that my cheap trainers have enough grip, and that my mind has enough focus to follow, because the only alternative is

219

clambering back into Godfrey's room and getting myself murdered.

Out I go, over the rust-coloured roof tiles, all the while trying to ignore Godfrey shouting behind me. I notice a beam of light chasing me from the garden, and manage to look around to see Douglas Chappell himself wielding a torch and shouting at me to come down.

'I've called the police!' he bellows, and I gulp in terror.

'Keep going, Wilco!' Kesia whispers, and I can't help but feel guilty that I'm slowing her down. If she was on her own, she'd no doubt be hot-footing it to freedom right now. How much training has she had for situations like these? And how much work do I have to do to be even half as good as her?

My feet find their grip on the tiles, and eventually I've rounded the corner of the house so that the torchlight can't find me any more. We're at the side of the house, still on a sloping part of the roof, and the only thing keeping me going is imagining that I'm rock-climbing without a harness and what lies below me is a 200-metre drop. I have no option but to keep going, to try and follow Kesia's self-assured steps, as I find my way around and on to another flat portion of roof, where she has stopped and is waiting for me.

'Just forget about everyone else,' Kesia says as I find her again, her hands clamping down on both my

220

shoulders to stop them from shaking. 'My car is just down there. We're going to have to jump down now, and when you land, forget about absolutely anything and everything, except for getting up and running. I'm going to run ahead of you and get the car started. You just have to get through the gap in the fence, OK? My car will be there.'

'OK,' I reply, even though I'm very much not OK.

Kesia looks at me, worried, and slaps hard on both my arms as if to reassure me before she makes to get away. I nod to indicate that I understand, but really my mind is floating far away from my body. I'm almost certain that this can't be real, that none of this is happening.

As if to make everything worse, Godfrey's head pokes out from a nearby window. He daren't come outside, but he doesn't seem to have any problem yelling and swearing at me anyway.

'I see you, Wilco! Don't think I don't! You're going to pay for this, you arsehole!'

Kesia gives me one final look, her eyebrows furrowed with concern, before launching herself off the roof and to the ground below. I look down and watch her land – it's as if she's had aeons of gymnastics training – and she drops and rolls like an elegant acrobat before springing back to her feet and dashing away. Wow. Who would have guessed that the stupendously shy girl who's been following us around at school, chewing on her own ponytail, was capable of moves like that? Eddie's not going to believe it when I tell him. *If* I'm even alive at the end of this to be able to tell him.

I jump. Not the wondrously graceful jump that Kesia manages – my version involves sitting on the edge of the roof and letting my legs hang down before I drop – but I do it. My heart is beating so hard that I swear it's going to propel itself up my throat and right out of my mouth. And for a moment, a tiny moment, I get a sense of something just out of my grasp. Something teasing me from a dark part of my brain, something that's been bothering me right from the beginning of all this. I remember being up on the roof of the school, trying to fly, and even though I was scared then, the urgency just wasn't quite there. The powerful hit of adrenaline that I'm feeling now, that feeling that I might actually die in this very moment, gives me a flicker of an idea of what I might one day be capable of. I can feel it too; in those nanoseconds between me dropping through the air and landing there's a tiny flame of understanding. That I can't fly – I know that – but there's something else, something just out of reach that slows my fall and gives me a softer landing. It's there, just in front of me, and just out of reach, but it's definitely there. I make a mental note to remember this precise moment and this exact feeling, a snapshot of experience, so that I can try and recreate it another time.

Standing now, and regaining my sense of space and balance, I find myself back on the driveway, on the opposite side to where there's that gap in the railings, just past the trees. I can't see Kesia; she must have dashed off to wherever she's parked her car, but the front door is opening to my side and I know that I don't have long.

My lungs still blissfully free of any trace of asthma, I start the dash of my life, charging with all the energy I can muster to the other side of the house, where the gap is, because the front gates are still closed and I know that I haven't got the strength or ability to throw myself over them. I have to cross the open front door, where the female members of the Chappell family are standing but not daring to cross the threshold, and I briefly wonder where Godfrey and his father have got to, and why they aren't with them. But I haven't got any time to check. I don't even look to my sides as I go. I just push my head forward in front of me and will my legs to work as hard as they can.

I'm nearly there. I can see my escape route through the conifers, barely noticeable unless you know that it's there, and I keep going, trying to ignore the desperate screams coming from Mrs Chappell and her daughter, while also ignoring the nagging that's coming from one part of my brain, warning me to be on the lookout because Godfrey and his dad must be somewhere near. But that almost doesn't matter, because I'm nearly there. *I can do it, I can make it, just a little bit further and I'm there.*

A bolt of sudden heat flashes through my entire body. Hot and cold all at once, I freeze and look down to my side. Two tiny prongs are stabbing me, both attached to wires that feed back into a device being held by Douglas Chappell. I shiver with the electricity and feel my jaw chatter and spasm. The pain comes not directly from the prongs themselves, but from the fact that every single muscle in my body is contracting and contorting, until I have to fall to the ground with an ugly thud. I don't feel it; I don't feel anything at all, as I realise with a quirk of awareness, *So this is what being tasered feels like*, just as the world goes dark.

17

I'm in a room. Maybe a basement? It's dark and cold and I can feel clammy walls around me. No, not a base-ment...the ceiling is gabled. It's an attic. As my eyes adjust to the dark I find I can make out a skylight, and beyond it a night sky. I'm handcuffed to something... could be a pipe. Something heavy and solid enough to keep me from going anywhere. This room has damp, probably coming in from the roof. I can feel it. In the darkness I can sense so many things, like the shape of the space, the heaviness of the boxes that are stored up here and the distinct lack of soft furnishings. It's an attic space, but it's not lived in. Judging from the dust and cobwebs I can sense, I'd guess that nobody comes up here very often.

How did I get here? I can feel in my shoulders that I was heaved up and dragged. I think of Douglas Chappell pulling me up under the arms, with Godfrey holding my legs. I don't remember it happening exactly – I must have been completely out of it – but I can imagine it easily.

Even with his broken hand, Godfrey's still strong enough. And mean enough too.

Does he know what his father is up to? Being a school bully is one thing, but colluding on corruption of this scale is just horrible.

I pull at the handcuffs, trying to make sense of where I am and what I can do. Whatever it is I'm attached to, it's not letting me go anywhere, and the more I tug, the more I can feel the metal digging into my wrists. Damn it.

Where's Kesia? Did she make it to her car? Is she coming back to save me? I quickly realise that I shouldn't count on it. She was annoyed enough at me as it was. Plus, without any way to get in touch with Kesia or anyone else, I guess I should probably focus my energies on getting myself out of my own mess.

A stretch of bright light is cast against the gloom as a door opens at the bottom of a stairwell that leads up to this space. There are voices below: the unmistakable bellow of Douglas Chappell, and the lighter, colder voice of a woman. His wife perhaps?

'I said, "Go to bed!"' orders Chappell. 'I'll deal with this!'

'But the boy!' the woman says. 'He broke in! Why aren't you calling the police?'

'I'm sure it's just one of Godfrey's friends pulling a prank. It's late, and if I call the police then we'll have reporters all over us. We'll just keep the boy here until morning, and then sort it out with the right people then. Don't worry.'

He's trying to sound calm for the sake of his wife, saying it just so she won't interfere, but there's an undercurrent of something darker happening too, something that suggests that he knows more than he's letting on. I gulp back in fear and instinctively shrink away from the light, hunkering back into the deeper shadows behind me.

The stairs creak as Douglas Chappell, a man I'd only seen on the television and in the newspapers before today, comes up them. With the light from below behind him, he appears first in silhouette, but his features soon become clear, and become clearer still when he tugs on a cord that turns on the light. Behind him is Godfrey, like a scaled-down version of his father, or an echo of what his father used to look like. Where Douglas's black hair is cropped and gelled back, Godfrey's is longer and sweeping. Godfrey's face is rounder, as though he's not quite grown out of his teenage puppy fat. The angles of Douglas's nose and jaw are sharper, whittled by age and stress.

'He's definitely the one?' The father asks his son as they both stand before me.

'Definitely. Be careful – he can move things with his mind. He's dangerous. Just look at what he did to my hand!' Godfrey replies, holding his plaster cast up before him as if in evidence. No mention of how he had beaten

227

me to pieces just before, and how I was only protecting myself from further violence. But I remember the tension and the crunch of his bones, and I shudder.

'Well, come on, what were you doing here then?' At first I don't realise that he's even talking to me, but another brusque 'Come on!' soon jolts me to awareness. Did either of them even see Kesia? Is she running free with the flash drive without them even knowing?

'Just a prank,' I say, echoing Douglas's own explanation to his wife.

'Bull,' the man responds quickly. 'You're working with them, aren't you?'

'Who?'

'Don't "who" me, kid. You know very well who. The Vigils. They put you up to this. What is it, some kind of field assignment to prove your mettle? Get the dirt on Chappell and get promoted? Taking one for the team, are you?'

'No!' I start. 'I was just here getting Indira's phone back!'

'Dad,' Godfrey interjects. Is he nervous that I might spill the beans on his sordid blackmailing? 'He's a little moron, but he's not a Vigil.'

'Shut up, Godfrey.'

'Seriously, Dad, he's the biggest loser in my school. Just a random scholarship kid. Doesn't even have any friends.'

'I think –' Douglas turns to Godfrey, looking and sounding as if he wants to teach his son an important lesson – 'this "little moron" of yours knows more than he's letting on. Thought he could get to me through you, no doubt, and presumed that nobody would suspect a ridiculous teenager. But if he's got powers, then he's one of them. The Vigils get in early, using their psychic trackers to find them, and recruiting them before anyone else has a chance.'

'No!' I try, but neither seems to really be listening to me. 'I'm just here for the phone, I promise!'

'But, Dad, the Vigils work for you, don't they? Why are you talking like they're the bad guys?'

'Get downstairs, Godfrey,' Douglas instructs, his tone shifting suddenly. It sounds like whatever it is he's been mulling in his head, he's finally made up his mind.

'No, but, Dad—'

'I SAID, "GET DOWNSTAIRS!"'

The sudden explosion of rage gives me an added jolt of fear, my heart rate becoming an audible pressure in my ears.

Godfrey backs away to the staircase, but he's not happy about it. I don't know what's worse for him – that he was yelled at so harshly, or that it was right in front of me. There's something else in his expression too, a vague sense of worry. Is he concerned about me? Mad and bad Godfrey Chappell, king of Gatford House? Is it about

Indira's phone? Or is he more worried about what I might do to his father? I broke Godfrey's bones without even trying; what else could I do to get myself out of here?

There's a trunk to one side of the attic; old-fashioned and thick with dust. Douglas goes over to it, his hands balled into uncomfortable, white-knuckled fists, his gaze constantly flickering back as if to check that I'm really still there and that I haven't run off. As if I could, handcuffed to what I now can see is a pipe attached to the boiler system. I pull at it again and look up and along to see if there is any loose join I could work at. One end of the piping reaches down through the floorboards, the other into the pressure tank. The metal clangs as I tug.

From the trunk, Douglas retrieves something wrapped in a stretch of felt-like fabric. I feel it out with my mind, trying to work out what the shape is and what this object could possibly have to do with me, frustrated that although I can see and feel things, seeing *through* things is one boundary I can't cross. I might as well be wearing a blindfold. I remember when I was being tested by Dr Starr, and the frustration I felt when I disappointed him. I'm feeling that same frustration now. Whatever is under that fabric is as hidden to my mind as it is to my plain sight. It's heavy though. Heavier than I would expect.

It's a gun. The fabric falls away and it glints under the bare light bulb.

What the hell? He can't seriously be thinking of killing me – he's a politician for God's sake! I reckon that it has to be a replica or a really old gun, something antique and useless. He wants to scare me. That must be it. And yet, it's a gun. Definitely a gun. How the heck did I end up in this mess?

'You shouldn't be interfering with things that you don't understand,' Douglas seethes.

'I haven't been interfering with anybody! I was just getting the phone for Indira! Please! I don't know anything else!' Desperately I try to yank the gun out of his hand with my mind, but I can't seem to concentrate. As the adrenaline starts to pump through me once again, the room around us seems to twist and rock, as though the house were being battered by a gale outside. Is that me? I can't focus; instead all the energy in me feels as if it's seeping out and all around, like before with the house alarm.

'Stop that!' Douglas yells. 'Whatever it is you're doing, stop it!'

But I can't. He doesn't know it, but the truth is that I am in way over my head here. I'm scared, and even though I'm tied up and not even moving, I can't seem to catch my breath.

I wonder if it's possible that this is where I'm going to die. My life will barely be a footnote, and my mum will be alone. I can't do that. I can't leave her alone. I've been working too hard for it to come to this. I've got to do something, anything, to get myself out of this mess.

'Indira! She'll be wondering where I am! I was meant to check in with her! She'll tell you, I was only here for the phone! She'll tell you!'

'I think you've underestimated the mess you're in, young man. And don't think I don't know that a bint like that Indira girl will say and do anything to get herself out of trouble,' Douglas sneers.

'Please!' I yell. 'I'm nothing! I don't know anything! I'm small fry!'

'What kind of fool do you think I am, kid? I bet you were in my office. And I know you and your Vigil friends have been itching to get a piece of me.' He's pointing the gun at me. It seems like such a stupid metal thing, but in my anxious state, I just can't seem to get a firm hold on it. 'Tell me the truth, right now. Tell me everything, and I won't press charges for burglary.'

I want to calm down, I seriously do. But it's too late for all that now. The shuddering around us is getting worse. Just seconds earlier it was barely even noticeable, but now it feels like the floorboards beneath us have turned to jelly. In my heightened state I find my mind looking around and locking on to objects, feeling them out and touching. Touching and feeling everything around me in an endless cycle of panic and desperation. But most stuff in here is too heavy, and anyway, before I can focus, my thoughts flit to the next thing – looking and locking and touching with my mind-hands. It's crazy and it's frightening, but as I panic, things seem to be moving of their own accord anyway. It's like an earthquake, with the epicentre being my own brain.

Douglas looks around, scared and confused as the rumbling steps up a gear.

'I said, "Stop it!" Stop it at once!'

'I can't!' I force out through gritted teeth.

'You'll wake up the whole damn neighbourhood!'

'I'm scared!'

He aims, as if he can frighten me into putting a halt on things. He doesn't seem to realise that the more he threatens and scares me, the worse the earthquake is going to get.

'Dad?' Godfrey's comes back up the stairs. 'What the hell is going on? Everything is shaking! Mum is scared!'

I catch a glimpse of Godfrey's face briefly, and think I must be starting to hallucinate, because for some reason he looks about four years old. The same age I was when I first saw my own father for what he really was . . .

The mix of the shaking and the reappearance of his son seems to have some effect on Douglas, like he has no idea what he's meant to do next, and then something bangs.

I feel it. I can feel the gun, solid and heavy, shining and hot, and I know right there and then that it's real. There's

233

no time for Douglas to aim elsewhere. I don't think he actually even meant to pull the trigger, but that doesn't matter now. Because I can see the bullet. It's charging out like a spitball of molten metal, flying at a million miles an hour right at me.

I squeeze my eyes shut, but the bullet is still there, shattering its way through the space between us, echoing throughout the chasm that is this dank and dusty loft space, and I find that I can touch it. More than that, I can hold it. My mind doesn't seem to care about the charge or the velocity; it's quite comfortable just grabbing at it. And even as the bullet heads straight for me, I find that I can look all the way around it, as if it's travelling in slow motion, like a motion-capture freeze frame.

When I open my eyes the bullet is right up near my face, on target to charge through my skull and continue beyond, but it's stopped. I'm holding it, right there, and suddenly I realise that it's a silly little thing. I frown, and it drops to the floor right by my feet.

In that sudden moment of clarity, it's like a switch has been clicked in my brain. No more shaking, and no more panic. All that energy I was feeling crystallised in my catching of the bullet, and now the gun is no longer a threat.

'Dad . . .' Godfrey mutters.

Douglas Chappell is still like a statue, frozen in horror. I'm pretty stunned too, but I don't have time to dwell on anything. I just want to get out of here; I *need* to get out of here!

'What the hell, Dad?' Godfrey says again, coming over to his father, who is still holding the gun, and still pointing it right at me. 'Put that down!'

'Godfrey!' I yell, realising that loyalties are shifting, that as awful as he is, Godfrey was probably not prepared to see his father murder one of his classmates.

'I . . . I . . .' Douglas stutters, realising the same thing, looking at Godfrey and seeking to defend himself. 'I didn't even know it was still loaded. I didn't know!'

'Dad, what's going on? What did you just *do*?'

I have to test that it's not me holding Douglas Chappell frozen in place, because he seems completely unable to move. He keeps muttering about the gun, about it being an old war antique, and how it must have been more sensitive than he thought.

Crazy as it seems, it's Godfrey who retrieves the gun, wraps it gingerly back in the felt cover and puts it back away in the trunk. Then he finds the key to the handcuffs and sets me free. His good hand shakes as he does it, and his plaster-casted hand is clumsy with the effort, but soon enough the handcuffs fall away and I'm able to get to my feet again.

We don't notice the roaring outside until it's right on top of us. It's like a thunderstorm, painful and deafening.

Godfrey dashes over to the skylight and opens it,

poking his head out to see what's causing the almighty noise.

'A helicopter!' he exclaims, but I can barely hear him. 'Vigils!'

I turn back to the attic and see that Douglas has gone, and I presume that he's run away back down into the house. I start to head over to the stairs to make my exit too, but Godfrey calls out to me: 'Not that way! My dad's got security! They'll be down there!'

'Then where?' I ask, baffled.

Godfrey grabs a sturdy box to stand on, pushes the skylight wider, and starts to clamber out.

'What are you doing?' I yell, but I don't think he can hear me. The helicopter must be right above us.

I can't believe I'm climbing out of a window for the second time this evening, but I do it. The roof isn't steep, and my trainers seem to be gripping well on to the tiles. We sit and shuffle along, me following Godfrey, as if he might know an easy way down.

The helicopter is right above us, and pummels us with a downdraught. I can't even look up, and my eyes squint and water in the wind. Godfrey tries to shout something at me, but I can't hear him. I can barely open my eyes to see him.

Slowly the helicopter, which I can now see is emblazoned with the Vigil logo, turns in the air and moves across to hover above the vast expanse of the Chappells' lawn. It's going to land in the garden, and I have to get out there. As it touches down and the rotors slow, the battering of wind around us ceases and I'm able to talk to Godfrey once again.

'Don't say anything.' He stops me before I even manage to start. 'Whatever happens, we're not talking about this evening ever again. It never happened.'

'Come with me,' I say, tilting my head over to where the helicopter has landed, to where Kesia has now appeared.

'This never happened,' Godfrey repeats sharply.

His face is pale and stricken, completely undone with the shock of witnessing his father's true colours. Godfrey might be a brutal bully, but no one deserves to see his father like that. I'm remembering my own father. I'm remembering peering out through a crack from behind my nearly closed bedroom door, looking at him looming over Mum as she cowered on the sofa. I remember the fear I felt, wondering if I would always be so small and weak, wondering if he would ever turn his anger on me, and then wishing he would, just so that he'd stop yelling at her. But I stayed there in my room, behind the door. They must have thought I was asleep, but the truth is I never slept through it. The truth is I would pray for the Vigils to arrive and save us every single time my father lost his temper. Quantum, with his brute strength and silver suit, followed by his second-in-command, Deep Blue, would appear at my door and my dad would be the one who was afraid.

237

Hayley Divine would speed in and scoop Mum up and whisk her to safety while the Red Rose would come to me, quaking on my bed, and hold me close until I stopped crying. The Vigils never came, not then, no matter how hard I prayed.

But they're here now.

My body seems to know what I'm about to do before my brain does. I stand up and creep forward across the roof tiles so that I'm standing right on the edge of the house, my toes tipping into the gutter. Instead of feeling outwards with my mind-hands, I feel inwards instead. I feel my own body, the weight of it and the pressure pulsing through my veins. It's strange how calm I feel, like everything I've gone through over the last few weeks has been building to this very moment, and now that I'm here I can't believe that it ever scared me so much.

I jump.

I can't fly, but I can support myself just enough to stop my fall being catastrophic. My own mind cradles my body, the physical cocooned by the mental. It's not flying, it's telekinesis, but instead of all my energy being focused on something else, it's me that I'm holding, me that I'm feeling, and me that I'm supporting.

The garden lawn comes up to greet me, and I drop and roll, exhausted by the effort.

18

I feel better once I remember how to breathe.

Weirdly, the instinct to reach for my inhaler is still there, like a reflex. I pat down the pockets of my trousers, expecting it to be there, but instead I feel the phone, still safely stowed away. I place one hand over my heart, feeling it beating wildly under my ribcage, but gradually slowing down, slowly realising that the worst is finally over and that I'm safe now.

I'm in the helicopter. Kesia fixes the straps around me and places the headset over my ears so that I have a chance to hear what's going on. The large padded headphones muffle the noise of the rotary blades whirring above, but Kesia's voice is loud and clear, fed through from the microphone on her headset.

'You good?' she asks.

I nod at her, before realising that I have a microphone too.

'I'm fine!' I say. 'What about Godfrey?'

'The ground crew have him. Don't worry, he's safe.'

'And Douglas Chappell?'

'We've got him. I've given the flash drive to the right people. It has exactly what we needed. His career is over. We did good. Are you all right?'

I'm surprised at her tone. Is she including me in that? No, that would be impossible. It must be the headset and the microphone. Even with them cushioning the noise, the constant drone of the helicopter is oppressive.

'Are you even listening to me?' Kesia shouts, clicking her fingers in front of my face to get my attention.

'Yeah, sorry,' I say.

'Don't think you're getting away with this stunt just because you ended up getting yourself out again in one piece. It doesn't work like that, and you're still in big trouble. If you ever get to be part of the team, you've got to learn how to listen to your superiors, to hold back and follow orders!'

'There's a chance that I might get to be a part of the team one day?' I grin at her.

I'm looking out of the window, and the night lights of Gatford town paint the whole place in shades of brown and orange. The cars on the nearby motorway are dual rivers of white and red. With my nose pressed up against the glass I can work out where the High Street is, and then from there, I can just about make out my road, but the helicopter leans and turns before I can spot my own house. They're not taking me home. I guess that means that we're going to London and the HQ. Kesia might be done ticking me off, but something tells me I'm still in for a long night yet. Kesia, an undercover agent for the Vigils – who would have thought?

I think about Eddie and my heart squeezes with a pang.

'You're not coming back to Gatford House, are you?' I say to her.

'Not now that my cover is blown, no.'

'I don't think they saw you there. And I wouldn't say anything...'

'I already did secondary school, and I'm not going through it again if I can help it.'

'Eddie will miss you...'

I'm not even sure if this is a conversation that I should be having, not while Eddie's still completely clueless about Kesia's real identity, but just in case this is the last chance I get to see her, before she disappears into the Vigils' world, I feel like I need to do something for my best mate. He deserves it.

She lets out a long deep breath and doesn't say anything. I can tell that this conversation isn't easy for her, but that doesn't mean that I'm letting her off.

'I mean, would it be so bad if you told him who you really are?'

'Don't.' Kesia sighs. 'Look, Eddie's very sweet, but it was never going to happen.'

'Eighteen is only three years older than fifteen...'

'But doing what I do and knowing what I know, it's also a million miles away. I know that Eddie likes drama, but I don't think he needs *this* kind of drama in his life.'

'Are you at least going to say goodbye?'

She looks at me, her lips pressed together. She doesn't answer. I drop it.

I wish I wasn't so tired. Don't some people dream of flying in helicopters, and spend tons of money for the privilege? I just want to go to sleep. I'm exhausted. Perhaps if I closed my eyes for just a second it would be all right. It's not as if I could actually sleep in here, what with all the noise and excitement. And yet, my eyelids are heavy, and Kesia's gone back to looking out of her own window, and surely I'm allowed to be a little tired after everything that has happened tonight? It was only a few weeks ago that lifting Mr Slim was enough to wipe me out, and now look at where I am: stopping speeding bullets and not-quite-but-nearly flying? I have to give my body time to adjust, which is why I'm certain that closing my eyes right now, just for a little bit, would probably be OK.

I wake up when the helicopter comes to a stop on the landing pad.

'Come on, sleepyhead.' Kesia playfully punches me on the arm. 'The night's not over yet!'

Around me is London, lit up bright and sparkling. I wish I knew my landmarks a little better, but I recognise the Eye on the Southbank, and laid out in front of it the shimmering Thames, like a dark rainbow of reflections. We're on the top of a building, I presume it's Vigil HQ, but there's no way to know for sure. Glancing up, the sky is still cloudless, although the stars are harder to pick out than they were in Gatford, and instead of inky dark, it's a nearly-black-but-rusty orange.

When I start to get up and out I find that my legs are sore, and once my feet hit solid ground I have to stretch out like I've never stretched before. I'm in one crazy contortion – one arm thrown over my head, and the other pushed out in front of me – when the man who was flying the helicopter opens his door and jumps down. He's wearing a navy Lycra suit, and under his headset a matching dark blue mask. I freeze as he takes the headset off, followed swiftly by the mask, and goes to muss up his curly hair, which has been flattened by the layers.

It's Deep Blue. I've been sitting directly behind Deep Blue and I didn't even know. And now here he is, standing right in front of me, and shaking himself out as if he too found the ride tiring and uncomfortable.

Seeing me watching him, Deep Blue steps forward and extends a hand. I look at the hand – it's a huge hand – like it's a strange and alien creature.

'Hi,' Deep Blue says.

Is he really speaking to me? I look behind me to make sure, but Kesia's gone off to talk to some other agents who have come out on to the helipad to welcome us. There's no one else. Deep Blue is looking right at me and I'm eight again, staring at his masked face in a poster, or running around our tiny flat in the replica costume Mum made me for my birthday.

'Hi?' I say back; at least, that's the sound I attempt to make. What actually comes out is more like a splutter.

I straighten myself out, and only then do I finally realise that the extended hand has a purpose and that I should be shaking it. Deep Blue laughs at me and my blustering, while inside I'm hating myself for being so awkward at such an important moment.

'I'm Lloyd,' he says.

'No, you're Deep Blue,' I reply.

He laughs. Deep Blue laughs.

'You can call me Lloyd,' he says.

'I didn't know it was you flying,' I say, almost apologetically. 'I didn't think the big guys like you came out on little trips like this.'

'Well, Agent Kittyhawk is a good pal of mine, and it sounded like she could use a ride.'

'I'm sorry that I caused so much trouble,' I say.

'Well, let's just be thankful that it all didn't end up much, much worse.'

'Hey, er . . . Deep Blue?'

244

'Lloyd.'

'Yeah...' Like I'm ever actually going to call him that. 'How old were you when you realised that you were different? And how did you know that you were going to be a hero?'

He starts walking towards where the other agents are standing waiting, and I walk with him.

'I was probably about your age,' he reveals. 'You been getting the headaches?'

'Hell, yeah. I mean, I haven't had one in a couple of weeks now, but they were awful.'

'Some of us get the headaches, some of us get other things. It's just part of the process. Anyway, after some skull-splitting headaches, I started to discover that my ability to retain information, and to work out things others couldn't, was becoming very pronounced. But it doesn't happen all at once. You don't just wake up one day with all this power and not knowing what to do with it. Can you imagine what that would be like? It would completely fry your brain.'

'Are you saying that I could get better at the whole telekinesis and psychic mind-eyes thing?'

'I'm saying that you probably don't yet know half of what you're capable of. I saw you soar through the air tonight. And what was that I was hearing about you stopping a bullet? That's pretty impressive stuff, you know? But don't forget the most important thing: just because you're super, that doesn't automatically make you a super*hero*. Being a hero comes from somewhere else entirely. Powers are the start of it, but it's what you do with them that counts. Understand?'

I nod as we reach the others. Kesia stands with her hands on her hips, holding back a scowl. I have a feeling that she wants to tell me off some more but doesn't because Deep Blue is standing so close. The other two agents, wearing sharp suits and ties, check me over before they enter the codes for the side doors and lead the way into the building.

I'm surprised at how little I remember from my last visit to the HQ. We all take the lift the whole way down to the bottom, deep underground, and Kesia and Deep Blue chat the whole time like they're old friends. They're discussing, of all things, the latest round of eliminations in some TV music talent show they're both watching. I'm baffled by just how normal they seem. When the lift doors open we emerge into what appears to be one long corridor, some parts tiled in an old-fashioned style, with modern steel bulkheads protruding at regular intervals. I didn't come down this deep on my last visit, but I recognise the architecture anyway.

'This was an old underground station,' Deep Blue says to me. 'It originally opened in 1907 and was called The Strand, named after the road that runs above us. Later, when it became a part of the Piccadilly line, it was known as Aldwych, but it eventually closed in the early nineties. The Vigils bought the property, and it's been our London base ever since, right under the heart of London.'

Wow. I knew that Deep Blue was more intelligent than anyone, but I had no idea that he was such a geek . . .

'We've made some modifications and expanded it where we could,' he continues, 'but it's also a Grade Two listed building, so there's only so much that can be adapted or changed.'

'Lloyd,' Kesia sighs, 'stop boring the kid.'

'I'm not boring him!'

Kesia turns to me: 'All that brain-smarts, and the guy just can't take a hint.'

I want to reply and say something about how much I'm enjoying the history lesson, but I can't quite get over the fact that Kesia is using his first name. She's calling him Lloyd like it's absolutely normal!

'You'll probably want to call your mum – where does she think you are tonight? Do you need a cover story?'

Damn it Kesia, don't bring up my mum here, not while Deep Blue is standing right next to me! I don't want him to think that I'm a baby. Maybe he's smiling because he's amused, or maybe it's because he's just in a good mood, I don't know. Either way, I'm embarrassed. What kind of superhero needs to report in to his mother?

'She thinks I'm at Eddie's house,' I tell Kesia. 'Maybe I could wait until the morning to call her.'

Kesia nods at me and doesn't push it any further.

We head onwards through double doors and down corridors; the place is a rabbit warren of rooms and passages, some sleek and modern, and some tiled in the old style. Finally we reach a set of doors that requires an elaborate code, and the agents (and Deep Blue) lead me through.

'This is the mission room,' Kesia explains, gesturing out over a vast cavern.

We're standing on some kind of platform, a balcony that has stairs leading down into what is obviously the belly of the Strand. It reminds me of a control room for a space mission, like you see in films, lots of banks of desks with computer terminals, and then on one wall ahead of us a vast screen, which is currently projecting what I think is an aerial view of London, the Thames a silver snake towards the bottom.

'It's a little quiet here right now,' Kesia explains. 'It is the middle of the night after all . . .'

She leads the way down the stairs, which rattle under her boots. I have to hold on to the rail as I follow her down, scared that I might trip over myself or miss a step. It's really quite dark in here (the walls, ceiling and floor are all black) but there are spotlights aimed at the array of desks and a general glow coming from that main screen.

At first I don't even notice the people. Kesia's right, there aren't many in here, and I guess the ones who are working are on night duty or something. They don't even bother looking around when Deep Blue comes down the stairs. Will there ever be a time when I'm not completely in awe of him, or are they all just pretending to be cool?

'I'll see you around, yes, Joseph?' he says, planting a large and heavy hand on one of my shoulders.

I can't pretend to be cool. I can't pretend anything right now. Deep Blue has his hand on my shoulder, and is looking right at me. He knows my name.

'Keep yourself out of trouble, OK?' he laughs (and he has a really deep laugh) at my obvious inability to form proper sentences in front of him, and gives Kesia an affectionate pat on the back before he leaves for one of the rooms that offshoot this one.

'OK, you can sit here,' Kesia says, leading me over to one of the empty desks. 'Sorry if things are a bit boring for a while, but I need to sort some stuff out before we go over processing and debriefing. Just stay put...and don't touch anything.'

I spin slowly in my chair, a beetle-like ergonomic thing that tilts all the way back if I lean too far. On each turn, I take in something new: the Vigil logos rotating on all the screensavers on the computers that aren't being used, the agents who accompanied us down from the helipad drinking out of Vigil branded mugs, and then, at a desk on the other side of the room, a small girl in a massive rainbow scarf staring intently at a file.

'Louise!' I call, relieved to see someone I recognise in here. I know that Kesia said to stay put, but I figure going over to another desk to say hello is allowed under the circumstances.

'Oh hey! Wilco!' Louise says as I approach.

'It's Joseph,' I correct her.

'You sure you don't want Wilco as your codename? No worries, I've got some other ideas for you anyway. What do you think of "Wonderboy"?'

'Could we just stick with Joseph for now? It's been a long evening...'

'Well then, Joseph. Sounds like you've been causing quite a bit of trouble tonight...'

'Oh man, tonight has been mental,' I say, leaning against her desk. 'I was just trying to do the right thing, but it all went so wrong.'

'Hey, we all do stupid things sometimes. Don't beat yourself up about it.'

'I feel like I'm about to get detention or something. Like everyone is cross with me. This isn't how I wanted it to be.'

'You'll be OK. And one day, I'll tell you about all the mischief and hijinks I got up to with Erica.'

'Erica?'

'Oh! Nobody's told you yet! I presumed you knew because you were having a chat with Lloyd without his mask...'

'What?'

'Your clearance has been bumped up! Well done kiddo, you're one of us now.'

'One of us? Like I'm an actual Vigil now?'

'Well, not quite, but nearly. At least, you're definitely on the way there. Look, take my advice, go slow. Don't rush anything. You've got the whole rest of your life to go on crazy adventures.

'*Anyway*, your clearance level! It basically means that you get to know all the secret identities. Someone really should have gone over this with you already, but I guess it's late, and they're probably going to wait for the morning crew to come in before explaining everything.'

'So who is Erica then?'

'That would be me!' She flies down from the gantry, bright and cheerful despite the late hour.

'Vega?' I stutter. I swear, if my life was a cartoon my jaw would be dislocating and hitting the floor right now. I wonder how long she's been standing up there watching me, and I feel embarrassed.

'Erica,' Louise corrects. 'The codenames and the whole secret-identity thing are great for the media and the fans, but you're one of us now, Joseph. Get used to it!'

'I've seen you on the TV...' I burble. God, I must sound so stupid.

'So what can you do?' She looks exactly how I thought she'd look behind that mask, wide-eyed and smiley, plus also ridiculously pretty. I can't quite believe that she's

251

talking to me, that she's paying me any attention at all. She's in another league entirely, even from Indira!

'Show her, Joseph,' Louise insists, snapping me out of my zombie-like awe.

'Oh, OK...right...'

I look around me and see a pen on Louise's desk. Giving my head a little shake to make sure that I'm alert and ready, I use my mind to feel the pen out, and then raise it up. Strange how this feels so easy now, when only recently it would have made me sweat with pressure. The pen hovers out between the three of us, and for a flourish, I make it twirl a little and write the word *Vega* in the air.

'Not bad!' Vega enthuses (I'm really not sure how I'm ever going to be able to call these people by their real names, it's just too strange). Her little impressed smile is encouraging, and I rotate the pen so that it's swirling little cartwheels over my upturned hand.

I don't notice when Vega brings her own hand up, but I definitely notice when she giggles and causes the pen to catch fire.

'Hey!' I call out, whipping my own hand out of the way of the heat and flames. As my concentration breaks, the pen falls to the floor, where it fizzles happily under Vega's magical flames.

'Yeah, hey!' Louise exclaims before pouting. 'That was one of my favourites!'

Apparently rugby is one of those sports that doesn't stop for rain. This is one of the things that I know now that I didn't know before. And why do I know this now? Because I'm currently standing with Eddie and about two hundred other Gatford House students on the sidelines of the rugby pitch, and I'm getting really rather wet.

We're not allowed to put umbrellas up because it might obscure the view for the people behind us, and because apparently, according to Mr Armstrong, the weather isn't that bad. Apparently he's played sports during the Bangladeshi monsoon season or something. It's the kind of rain that doesn't come down in any particular direction, but infuses and permeates everything the moment you step outside. Everything becomes damp, so I suppose umbrellas would be useless anyway. The only solution would be to stay indoors, but apparently that's not happening either. Attendance at the match against Queen's is mandatory, to demonstrate school spirit and pride. Also because it's been deemed by the staff (and Mr

Armstrong in particular) that our side needs as much cheering and support as we can possibly muster, in the hope that this will somehow outweigh the fact that Godfrey, our star player, is on the bench.

Godfrey is standing a little bit in front of me, his arms folded tight across his chest, and even though I can't see his face, I know that his scowl is hard and fixed. And to be perfectly honest, after everything he's been through, I feel sorry for him. I really do.

He's so emotionally involved with the game that he practically jumps with every huddle and throw. You can tell that his instinct is to be right up front and involved, and it must be killing him to have to watch from the sidelines. His good hand is set in a permanent fist, and his voice carries like thunder with every insult he hurls at the woefully inadequate Gatford players, as if that could have any impact.

It doesn't. We're losing abysmally. I personally have no idea of how or why this is – rugby is still a mystery to me despite years of PE lessons – but from what Eddie tells me, and from the sounds of the cheers from the Queen's supporters huddled across the pitch from us, we are losing. But not just losing, shamefully losing. It's a mortifying, excruciating massacre. I like to think that this isn't completely my fault, and that Godfrey brought all of this on himself, but the truth is that he was more than just the star player. He was the captain, the glue that held the fragile pieces together, and the mascot too. He represented success and hope and majesty, and without him out there on the field, the rest of the team is completely lost.

I might have no idea of what is happening, but I know it's bad. The sense of failure permeates almost as deeply as the rain. Everything is soggy and dismal.

And yet Godfrey hasn't stopped calling out and shouting for the entire match so far. He won't give up. He switches from insults to encouragement and back again with every fluffed pass and missed catch. He's utterly involved with this, and no matter how bleak this whole thing is looking, which is particularly bleak under this heavy grey sky, he's not giving up. He refuses to. Maybe school pride and grim determination are his superpowers?

He's still out here, and not in hiding. The last week has not been easy, especially for him. Whereas my life has gone back to relative normality, he's had to watch his father get arrested. Douglas Chappell MP, the man whose job it was to protect the Vigils, was revealed to be just about the most corrupt player in the game. The Ditko Finance scandal is the scoop of the century, and could change the way the government controls the Vigils in this country for ever.

All things considered, I've got off pretty lightly. For all anyone else knows, I'm just the same loser kid I always was, with a stupid little superpower that's barely even worth mentioning, save for the odd younger kid asking me to do a trick for them. The Vigils seem to have kept everything under control online and some of the teachers at Gatford are looking into instigating a vigorous anti-bullying policy, which is nice, I suppose. And it seems that nobody is particularly fussed about what I can do anyway. Floating stationery and shuttlecocks? Apparently not sexy enough for the teens of today. Godfrey hasn't told a soul about what happened in his attic, and for that I'm grateful. It's not like we're friends or anything – he's still a bully, after all, one who made my life hell and blackmailed Indira – but there's something there that wasn't there before. A truce? I don't want to risk jinxing it by giving it too much thought. I'm planning to enjoy my pain-free school life for as long as it can last.

The whistle goes for half-time, and a lot of the people around me start to move away to stretch their legs or walk off some of the bitter disappointment. I see a few go to beg the supervising teachers for permission to go and study in the library (that's how bad things are) but nobody is allowed. Normally a big game like this is one long party that everyone looks forward to, regardless of the weather or whether they care about sport, but today we're all drowning in shame.

'Oh dear,' says Eddie, shaking his head. 'It's painful to watch.'

He's holding up pretty well, considering that Kesia has

disappeared from the face of the earth. Sure, he was glum for a bit, and was a bit stunned when he found that her phone wasn't working any more, but he seems a lot better now. I would have preferred it if Kesia had been a little more honourable and explained everything to Eddie herself, but then again, maybe it's for the best. Clean break, total cut-off, cold turkey. Last I heard, she's on the other side of the world, having her adventures and barely thinking about us. I wish I could tell Eddie everything, but I also know that I can't. Maybe one day. Maybe never.

'Joseph?'

It's Indira. At first neither of us can react or say anything, but after an uncomfortable moment, Eddie decides that maybe he should go and join the others walking around.

'Hi,' I say as she comes right up to me.

Her dark hair has gone slightly fuzzy thanks to the rain, but she still looks supermodel-stunning.

'I've been trying to find the time to come and talk to you,' she says. 'But I've been so busy with everything.'

'No, I know. Of course you have.'

'And I wanted to say thank you, for getting that phone back to me.' She brings a hand up to push a strand of hair behind her ear. 'It was very noble of you to go through all of that for me. I hope I didn't get you into any trouble.'

'Sure. No problem, and no trouble. It all went down exactly as you said it would.'

'And I've also been thinking, you were so amazing about everything, and I've never really given you a chance before. You know?'

A beat where I'm not entirely sure whether I want to say anything. I look down at my feet, feeling hot and awkward.

'So I was wondering, perhaps we should do that coffee again, at the court in the shopping centre? We could spend some more time together? Or something?'

'Indira...'

I look up at her, and into her eyes. They're so beautiful, and so perfect, and looking directly back at me. It really wasn't so long ago that I would have killed for an opportunity like this, and even then I wouldn't have believed that it was possible in a million years. Looking back down at my feet again, I try to muster up some of what I felt before. Where is the blood boiling, and the heart racing, and the clammy hands? She's exactly where I want her to be, my wildest dreams are coming true right in front of my eyes, and yet...

'Look, Indira...' I start.

'I mean, sure, you don't have to give me an answer now or anything. I was only suggesting it, that it might be nice, as friends, or whatever...'

'Indira, I'm not sure that it would be a good idea.'

Because so much in my life has changed. Because I've gone and turned myself inside out over the last few weeks.

Because my priorities are nothing like what they were before. And because right now, in this new light, I'm not entirely sure she was ever who I thought she was. She's still beautiful, but there's something else too, something that makes her a little less perfect and a little more sour. She might have implied that she could be interested in me if I helped her by getting the phone back, but it's taken her this long to say anything to me. I don't think she was ever interested in me, not really. She just wanted something. She used me for homework, then used me to get her phone back, and even now, instead of feeling excited by being around her, I can't help wondering what it is she wants this time. I didn't think it would ever be possible to switch off the feelings I had for her, not after having them for so long, but here we are. She's not who I thought she was, and I guess I'm not who I thought I was either.

'Right.' I don't think she's used to rejection. And I'm certainly not used to being the one who's doing the rejecting.

'I mean, we can hang out in school and in class and stuff, but I just think that maybe it wouldn't be the best thing for us to see that much of each other outside of school.'

Was that too harsh? That feels like it was way too harsh. Where the hell has Eddie gone?

'No, no, no, of course. You're perfectly right. And I was only asking, you know, as friends and stuff.'

'Sure.' I stare at my feet in their horrible, cheap shoes, and for the first time in my life I find myself praying for the rugby match to start up again.

'Good. Well, that's that then!' She turns and walks away, and I try not to notice how red her face is, or how forced her smiles with her girlfriends seem.

That was horrible.

'What did Indira want?' Eddie asks, coming back over.

'Just some homework help,' I tell him.

'You going to do it for her?'

'Nope, not this time. And in fact, you know what? I think I'm going to let people do their own damn work from now on. No more *Wilco*. I've got my own stuff to worry about after all.'

'Good for you!' Eddie exclaims, clapping me firmly on the back. 'And how's your mum with everything?'

'Stressed. Worried. Wants to know where I am all the time.' Which is understandable, especially since I explained to her that I wasn't actually at Eddie's place the other night. She was upset, and she cried again, which I hated, but she calmed down a little bit once I showed her a selfie I had taken with Vega (all masked up to protect her true identity of course). I think she's coming round to the idea of me being a superhero. At least, I hope she is. I try not to tell her stuff unless I absolutely have to, but even she would admit that my powers come in handy sometimes. Like when doing the washing-up, or hanging laundry up to dry.

Half-time is over, and the crowds reassemble. Everybody's shoulders are hunched. Nobody wants to look at the pitch. It's just going to be another misery-fest, regardless of how much Godfrey is shouting and jeering. I wish I even had an inkling of what is going on, but despite Eddie trying his best to explain what's happening on a number of different occasions, all I ever see are monsters grown thick on protein shakes pummelling each other for the sake of a weirdly shaped ball.

I keep my eye on it, watching it pass between players (silently noting how many of the Gatford team have been mean to me over the years – the answer is all of them), thrown high, hooked low, before disappearing under arms and into scrums.

And then I feel the ball. I don't even register it at first – the sensation has become so natural for me. But there it is, in my mind and out there on the pitch.

I let go quickly, ashamed of myself for even thinking that I might be able to have some influence here. I am not a cheat, plus I have a feeling that our rugby team would rather lose honourably than win with my help. But if it's only one play... just one little nudge from me to make everyone feel a little better, would that be so bad? Would anyone really mind? Would anyone even *know*?

There goes another ball lost to the wrong end of the pitch. Next to me, Eddie buries his head in his hands.

'I can't watch any more...' he groans.

And then, out of nowhere, I'm standing up and screaming in a voice so unexpected that at first I'm not even sure that it's me saying it, 'COME ON, GATFORD! YOU CAN DO IT!'

My call resonates with the people around me, and I feel the ripples of energy like a stone hitting still water. Everyone, even Godfrey down in front, turns to look at me.

'Joseph, mate... you don't have to do this,' Eddie says, tugging on my blazer.

But I won't. I raise one fist high into the sky and I start to pump it, raising a thumping cry of 'GATFORD!' with every punch.

Soon everyone joins in. The whole of the crowd, even the teachers, is rallying. Both teams on the field stop briefly to watch as the Gatford pupils are stoked into a frenzy, fists thumping into the air with every loud syllable.

'GAT-FORD! GAT-FORD! GAT-FORD!'

One of our boys (it looks like William Prudent) is charging with the ball, driving himself forward fuelled by the chanting of his supporters, and I imagine pushing him further, an invisible wind at his back, forcing him across the field and out of the way of his enemies. Finally, he slams the ball down over the tryline, causing a riotous cheer from everyone gathered around me.

It wasn't cheating, I tell myself. *William would have scored with or without me…*

'A try!' Eddie yells at me, euphoric. 'We got a try!'

I'm not entirely certain what this means, but judging from the jumping and the cheering of everyone around me, I'm willing to bet that it's good.

What it seems to mean is that Gatford has a chance to kick the ball at the opposition's goalposts. There's still no way that we can win this game – we're way too far behind – but I feel the aura of the crowd as the boys on the field prepare, and they're jubilant. In front of me, Godfrey paces with tension, obviously desperate to get out on to the pitch and have his turn. This should be his kick, I can tell.

Once more, the ball is in my mind, even as one of our players steps back and takes aim. I can feel its rough leather surface, slick and wet with mud, and then it's in the air and rocketing forward. It's going to miss. We can all see that it's going to miss … except … A little nudge from me wouldn't be all that bad, would it?

Acknowledgements

Before everything, there is my family. My parents, Nigel and Elaine: none of this would be possible without your support, and your complete inability to ask me to pay any form of rent. My brother James, who has become one of the truest friends in my life as we've grown into adults, and my extended family too, particularly Grandma Jackie, and my uncle, aunts and cousins. As our family continues to grow larger I just become more and more proud and grateful that I have all of you in my life.

I owe so much to the team at Andersen Press. Charlie Sheppard and Chloe Sackur in particular, but also everyone else behind the scenes. It's your unwavering support and enthusiasm that has helped make my dream come true, not just once, but now twice. The journey that I've had with you all has been wonderful.

Bryony Woods, you are a dream literary agent. Having you on my side makes me feel that I can do absolutely anything in the world.

Whilst working on this book I have also ended up taking

some unexpected employment, and have found myself working with some amazing people in even more amazing places. At the risk of making things sound much more exciting and tantalising than they need to be, I'm afraid that I can't be more specific, but needless to say, you guys know who you are, and you all, in your weird and wonderful ways, have made a positive impact on *Wonderboy*'s journey. Thank you for all your support and encouragement.

To Gosh Comics in London, long may comic books always be a tax-deductible expense in the name of research! I love that my social life now pretty much revolves around you, and to the loyal members of the Capers group in particular, you have no idea how much you constantly inspire me and have helped shape my reading and research.

Endless thank yous to my Edgware Skcubrats and the staff of Edgware Starbucks (Skcubrats spelled backwards!) for providing me with motivation and coffee, and finally, to the fine folk of Twitter and Facebook (bloggers, writers, readers, and the rest!). There are far too many of you to name individually, but I love that I can count some of you as true friends. Spending endless hours in front of a computer screen can be isolating, but you make it sociable and fun. Thank you!

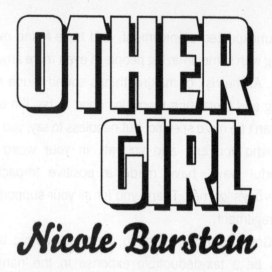

OTHER GIRL

Nicole Burstein

Longlisted for the Branford Boase Award

Louise and Erica have been best friends since forever.
Just one problem: Erica has superpowers. When Erica
isn't doing loop-the-loops in the sky or burning things
with her heat pulse powers, she needs Louise to hold her
non-super life together. But being a superhero's BFF is not
easy, and while Erica can fly faster than a speeding bullet,
she can't win every fight by herself.

'Suspenseful, comical and satirical'
Sunday Times

'*Othergirl* is a blast'
Matt Haig

9781783440610 £7.99